2018 最新題型

U0154250

NEW TOEIC
新多益一本通

【模擬試題】

★ 新多益六度滿分狀元
文之勤 著

★試題最逼真！

採2018全新制新多
益題型，共三回全
真試題，仿正式考
題開本大小與編排
方式，體驗正式上
場的真實感。

★規劃最用心！

六次新多益滿分狀
元文之勤老師親自
選題，囊括所有出
現頻率最高的主題
與單字，徹底掌握
新多益命題方向。

★解題最有效！

詳盡的試題翻譯與
解析，不錯過題目
中任何關鍵性單字
與文法，精準有效
解讀題目，快速找
出解題技巧。

★發音最專業！

新多益想拿高分首
重聽力，搭配專業
外師精心錄製的
MP3，熟悉各國不
同發音腔調，提前
做好應試準備。

英·美·加·澳
四國口音一次收錄

師德

Table of Contents

目錄

新多益測驗簡介

About TOEIC 測驗簡介

TOEIC 測驗全名為 Test of English for International Communication，也就是「國際溝通英語測驗」的簡稱，是專供母語非英語人士使用的英語能力測驗，報考者不限年齡、學歷；測驗分數反映受測者在國際生活及職場環境中的英語溝通能力。多益測驗並不要求一般生活及職場情境中常用英語以外的專業知識或字彙。

TOEIC 目前在全世界 120 多個國家施測，擁有 10,000 個以上的大型企業客戶、教育單位及政府機構，受測者一年約 600 萬人。TOEIC 不但在國內外各大企業界的人資部門被廣泛使用，作為企業員工英語能力管理工具、英語培訓績效檢驗標準、員工招募、升遷及外派人員篩選標準，在各校園中也常被用作大學推薦甄試入學、新生英語教學分班及診斷測驗、英語學習成就測驗及大學畢業英語門檻等用途。TOEIC 多益英語測驗也列為國內行政院公務人員英語檢測陞任評分計分標準對照表選項。

TOEIC 本身並沒有所謂的「通過」或「不通過」，而是客觀地將受測者的能力以聽力 5~495 分、閱讀 5~495 分、總分 10~990 分的指標呈現，提供各個機關人事決策的標竿，受測者也可以自評現在的英語能力，進而設定學習的目標。

📢)) 測驗方式

多益測驗為紙筆測驗，考生用鉛筆在電腦答案卷上作答。考生選好答案後，在與題目卷分開的答案卷上劃卡。答題時間約為兩小時，但考試時考生尚須先填寫個人資料，並簡短的回答關於教育與工作經歷的問卷，因此真正待在考場內時間會較長，約 2 小時 30 分鐘。測驗題數共 200 題，皆為單選題，分為兩大部分：**聽力與閱讀**。

〈聽力部分〉

◆ 測驗英語聽力理解的程度。

◆ 包含 4 大題，共 100 個單選題，以 CD 播放考題，考生會聽到各種模擬實境不同狀況的問題，以及相關主題的直述句、問句、對話以及獨白，然後根據所聽到的內容回答問題，測驗時間約為 45 分鐘。

題　型	題　數
照片描述	6 題
應答問題	25 題
簡短對話	39 題（13 段對話，每段對話包含 3 個問題）
簡短獨白	30 題（10 段獨白，每段獨白包含 3 個問題）

〈閱讀部分〉

◆ 測驗英文閱讀理解的程度。

◆ 分為 4 大題，共 100 個單選題，考生須閱讀多種題材的文章，並回答相關問題，考生可依個人能力調配閱讀及答題速度，測驗時間為 75 分鐘。

題　型	題　數
單句填空	30 題
短文填空	16 題
單篇文章理解	29 題（7~10 篇短文，每篇 2~5 題）
多篇文章理解	25 題（5 組短文，每組 5 題）

🔊 測驗內容

多益題型的設計，以職場的需要為主。測驗題的內容，從全世界各地職場蒐集而來，題材多元化，包含各種地點與狀況。

一般商務	契約、談判、行銷、銷售、商業企劃、會議
製造業	工廠管理、生產線、品管
金融／預算	銀行業務、投資、稅務、會計、帳單
企業發展	研究、產品研發
辦公室	董事會、委員會、信件、備忘錄、電話、傳真、電子郵件、辦公室器材、辦公室流程
人事	招考、雇用、退休、薪資、升遷、應徵與廣告
採購	比價、訂貨、送貨、發票
技術層面	電子、科技、電腦、實驗室與相關器材、技術規格
房屋／地產	建築、規格、購買、租賃、電力瓦斯服務
旅遊	火車、飛機、計程車、巴士、船隻、票務、時刻表、車站、機場廣播、租車、飯店、預訂、延遲與取消
聚會	商務／非正式午餐、宴會、招待、餐廳訂位
娛樂	電影、劇場、音樂、藝術、媒體
保健	醫藥保險、看醫生、牙醫、診所、醫院

🔊 測驗計分方式

多益考試分數由答對題數決定，再將每一部分（聽力、閱讀）答對題數轉換成分數，範圍分別在 5 到 495 分之間。兩部分加起來即為總分，分數範圍在 10 到 990 分之間。答錯不倒扣。答對題數與換算分數的對應請參閱以下對照表。

〈TOEIC 分數參考對照表〉

聽力部分		閱讀部分	
答對題數	換算分數範圍	答對題數	換算分數範圍
96~100	475~495	96~100	455~495
91~95	440~480	91~95	415~460
86~90	415~460	86~90	390~435
81~85	380~430	81~85	360~405
76~80	350~405	76~80	330~380
71~75	320~370	71~75	300~350
66~70	290~340	66~70	270~320
61~65	260~310	61~65	235~280
56~60	240~280	56~60	205~250
51~55	210~260	51~55	175~220
46~50	190~230	46~50	150~190
41~45	165~210	41~45	125~165
36~40	145~185	36~40	105~145
31~35	120~165	31~35	85~125
26~30	100~140	26~30	60~100
21~25	75~120	21~25	45~80
16~20	50~100	16~20	30~65
11~15	30~70	11~15	20~55
6~10	10~50	6~10	15~40
1~5	5~30	1~5	5~20
0	5	0	5

註：上述對照表格僅供參考，實際考試得分以官方成績為準。

📢 英語能力指標

多益測驗提供相當可信的語言能力測驗指標，得到不同的成績即代表擁有不同層級的英語語言能力，兩者間的對應請參閱以下對照表。

〈TOEIC 成績與英語能力參考對照表〉

TOEIC 成績	語言能力	證書顏色
905~990	英文能力十分近似於英語母語人士，能夠流暢有條理的表達意見、參與談話，主持英文會議，調和衝突並做出結論，語言使用上即使有瑕疵，亦不會造成理解上的困擾。	金色 (860 ～ 990)
785~900	可有效地運用英文滿足社交及工作上所需，措辭恰當、表達流暢；但在某些特定情形下，如：面臨緊張壓力、討論話題過於冷僻艱澀時，仍會顯現出語言能力不足的情況。	藍色 (730 ～ 855)
605~780	可以英語進行一般社交場合的談話，能夠應付例行性的業務需求，參加英文會議，聽取大部分要點；但無法流利的以英語發表意見、作辯論，使用的字彙、句型也以一般常見為主。	綠色 (470 ～ 725)
405~600	英文文字溝通能力尚可，會話方面稍嫌辭彙不足、語句簡單，但已能掌握少量工作相關語言，可以從事英語相關程度較低的工作。	棕色 (220 ～ 465)
255~400	語言能力僅僅侷限在簡單的一般日常生活對話，無法做連續性交談，也無法用英文進行工作。	
10~250	只能以背誦的句子進行問答而不能自行造句，尚無法將英文當作溝通工具來使用。	橘色 (10 ～ 215)

NEW TOEIC

Test 1

SAMPLE

TOEIC

MARKING DIRECTIONS

CORRECT MARK   INCORRECT MARKS

★ Use only pencil
★ Darken the circles completely
★ Erase cleanly

LISTENING SECTION

1 Ⓐ Ⓑ Ⓒ Ⓓ	26 Ⓐ Ⓑ Ⓒ Ⓓ	51 Ⓐ Ⓑ Ⓒ Ⓓ	76 Ⓐ Ⓑ Ⓒ Ⓓ
2 Ⓐ Ⓑ Ⓒ Ⓓ	27 Ⓐ Ⓑ Ⓒ Ⓓ	52 Ⓐ Ⓑ Ⓒ Ⓓ	77 Ⓐ Ⓑ Ⓒ Ⓓ
3 Ⓐ Ⓑ Ⓒ Ⓓ	28 Ⓐ Ⓑ Ⓒ Ⓓ	53 Ⓐ Ⓑ Ⓒ Ⓓ	78 Ⓐ Ⓑ Ⓒ Ⓓ
4 Ⓐ Ⓑ Ⓒ Ⓓ	29 Ⓐ Ⓑ Ⓒ Ⓓ	54 Ⓐ Ⓑ Ⓒ Ⓓ	79 Ⓐ Ⓑ Ⓒ Ⓓ
5 Ⓐ Ⓑ Ⓒ Ⓓ	30 Ⓐ Ⓑ Ⓒ Ⓓ	55 Ⓐ Ⓑ Ⓒ Ⓓ	80 Ⓐ Ⓑ Ⓒ Ⓓ
6 Ⓐ Ⓑ Ⓒ Ⓓ	31 Ⓐ Ⓑ Ⓒ Ⓓ	56 Ⓐ Ⓑ Ⓒ Ⓓ	81 Ⓐ Ⓑ Ⓒ Ⓓ
7 Ⓐ Ⓑ Ⓒ Ⓓ	32 Ⓐ Ⓑ Ⓒ Ⓓ	57 Ⓐ Ⓑ Ⓒ Ⓓ	82 Ⓐ Ⓑ Ⓒ Ⓓ
8 Ⓐ Ⓑ Ⓒ Ⓓ	33 Ⓐ Ⓑ Ⓒ Ⓓ	58 Ⓐ Ⓑ Ⓒ Ⓓ	83 Ⓐ Ⓑ Ⓒ Ⓓ
9 Ⓐ Ⓑ Ⓒ Ⓓ	34 Ⓐ Ⓑ Ⓒ Ⓓ	59 Ⓐ Ⓑ Ⓒ Ⓓ	84 Ⓐ Ⓑ Ⓒ Ⓓ
10 Ⓐ Ⓑ Ⓒ Ⓓ	35 Ⓐ Ⓑ Ⓒ Ⓓ	60 Ⓐ Ⓑ Ⓒ Ⓓ	85 Ⓐ Ⓑ Ⓒ Ⓓ
11 Ⓐ Ⓑ Ⓒ Ⓓ	36 Ⓐ Ⓑ Ⓒ Ⓓ	61 Ⓐ Ⓑ Ⓒ Ⓓ	86 Ⓐ Ⓑ Ⓒ Ⓓ
12 Ⓐ Ⓑ Ⓒ Ⓓ	37 Ⓐ Ⓑ Ⓒ Ⓓ	62 Ⓐ Ⓑ Ⓒ Ⓓ	87 Ⓐ Ⓑ Ⓒ Ⓓ
13 Ⓐ Ⓑ Ⓒ Ⓓ	38 Ⓐ Ⓑ Ⓒ Ⓓ	63 Ⓐ Ⓑ Ⓒ Ⓓ	88 Ⓐ Ⓑ Ⓒ Ⓓ
14 Ⓐ Ⓑ Ⓒ Ⓓ	39 Ⓐ Ⓑ Ⓒ Ⓓ	64 Ⓐ Ⓑ Ⓒ Ⓓ	89 Ⓐ Ⓑ Ⓒ Ⓓ
15 Ⓐ Ⓑ Ⓒ Ⓓ	40 Ⓐ Ⓑ Ⓒ Ⓓ	65 Ⓐ Ⓑ Ⓒ Ⓓ	90 Ⓐ Ⓑ Ⓒ Ⓓ
16 Ⓐ Ⓑ Ⓒ Ⓓ	41 Ⓐ Ⓑ Ⓒ Ⓓ	66 Ⓐ Ⓑ Ⓒ Ⓓ	91 Ⓐ Ⓑ Ⓒ Ⓓ
17 Ⓐ Ⓑ Ⓒ Ⓓ	42 Ⓐ Ⓑ Ⓒ Ⓓ	67 Ⓐ Ⓑ Ⓒ Ⓓ	92 Ⓐ Ⓑ Ⓒ Ⓓ
18 Ⓐ Ⓑ Ⓒ Ⓓ	43 Ⓐ Ⓑ Ⓒ Ⓓ	68 Ⓐ Ⓑ Ⓒ Ⓓ	93 Ⓐ Ⓑ Ⓒ Ⓓ
19 Ⓐ Ⓑ Ⓒ Ⓓ	44 Ⓐ Ⓑ Ⓒ Ⓓ	69 Ⓐ Ⓑ Ⓒ Ⓓ	94 Ⓐ Ⓑ Ⓒ Ⓓ
20 Ⓐ Ⓑ Ⓒ Ⓓ	45 Ⓐ Ⓑ Ⓒ Ⓓ	70 Ⓐ Ⓑ Ⓒ Ⓓ	95 Ⓐ Ⓑ Ⓒ Ⓓ
21 Ⓐ Ⓑ Ⓒ Ⓓ	46 Ⓐ Ⓑ Ⓒ Ⓓ	71 Ⓐ Ⓑ Ⓒ Ⓓ	96 Ⓐ Ⓑ Ⓒ Ⓓ
22 Ⓐ Ⓑ Ⓒ Ⓓ	47 Ⓐ Ⓑ Ⓒ Ⓓ	72 Ⓐ Ⓑ Ⓒ Ⓓ	97 Ⓐ Ⓑ Ⓒ Ⓓ
23 Ⓐ Ⓑ Ⓒ Ⓓ	48 Ⓐ Ⓑ Ⓒ Ⓓ	73 Ⓐ Ⓑ Ⓒ Ⓓ	98 Ⓐ Ⓑ Ⓒ Ⓓ
24 Ⓐ Ⓑ Ⓒ Ⓓ	49 Ⓐ Ⓑ Ⓒ Ⓓ	74 Ⓐ Ⓑ Ⓒ Ⓓ	99 Ⓐ Ⓑ Ⓒ Ⓓ
25 Ⓐ Ⓑ Ⓒ Ⓓ	50 Ⓐ Ⓑ Ⓒ Ⓓ	75 Ⓐ Ⓑ Ⓒ Ⓓ	100 Ⓐ Ⓑ Ⓒ Ⓓ

READING SECTION

101 Ⓐ Ⓑ Ⓒ Ⓓ	126 Ⓐ Ⓑ Ⓒ Ⓓ	151 Ⓐ Ⓑ Ⓒ Ⓓ	176 Ⓐ Ⓑ Ⓒ Ⓓ
102 Ⓐ Ⓑ Ⓒ Ⓓ	127 Ⓐ Ⓑ Ⓒ Ⓓ	152 Ⓐ Ⓑ Ⓒ Ⓓ	177 Ⓐ Ⓑ Ⓒ Ⓓ
103 Ⓐ Ⓑ Ⓒ Ⓓ	128 Ⓐ Ⓑ Ⓒ Ⓓ	153 Ⓐ Ⓑ Ⓒ Ⓓ	178 Ⓐ Ⓑ Ⓒ Ⓓ
104 Ⓐ Ⓑ Ⓒ Ⓓ	129 Ⓐ Ⓑ Ⓒ Ⓓ	154 Ⓐ Ⓑ Ⓒ Ⓓ	179 Ⓐ Ⓑ Ⓒ Ⓓ
105 Ⓐ Ⓑ Ⓒ Ⓓ	130 Ⓐ Ⓑ Ⓒ Ⓓ	155 Ⓐ Ⓑ Ⓒ Ⓓ	180 Ⓐ Ⓑ Ⓒ Ⓓ
106 Ⓐ Ⓑ Ⓒ Ⓓ	131 Ⓐ Ⓑ Ⓒ Ⓓ	156 Ⓐ Ⓑ Ⓒ Ⓓ	181 Ⓐ Ⓑ Ⓒ Ⓓ
107 Ⓐ Ⓑ Ⓒ Ⓓ	132 Ⓐ Ⓑ Ⓒ Ⓓ	157 Ⓐ Ⓑ Ⓒ Ⓓ	182 Ⓐ Ⓑ Ⓒ Ⓓ
108 Ⓐ Ⓑ Ⓒ Ⓓ	133 Ⓐ Ⓑ Ⓒ Ⓓ	158 Ⓐ Ⓑ Ⓒ Ⓓ	183 Ⓐ Ⓑ Ⓒ Ⓓ
109 Ⓐ Ⓑ Ⓒ Ⓓ	134 Ⓐ Ⓑ Ⓒ Ⓓ	159 Ⓐ Ⓑ Ⓒ Ⓓ	184 Ⓐ Ⓑ Ⓒ Ⓓ
110 Ⓐ Ⓑ Ⓒ Ⓓ	135 Ⓐ Ⓑ Ⓒ Ⓓ	160 Ⓐ Ⓑ Ⓒ Ⓓ	185 Ⓐ Ⓑ Ⓒ Ⓓ
111 Ⓐ Ⓑ Ⓒ Ⓓ	136 Ⓐ Ⓑ Ⓒ Ⓓ	161 Ⓐ Ⓑ Ⓒ Ⓓ	186 Ⓐ Ⓑ Ⓒ Ⓓ
112 Ⓐ Ⓑ Ⓒ Ⓓ	137 Ⓐ Ⓑ Ⓒ Ⓓ	162 Ⓐ Ⓑ Ⓒ Ⓓ	187 Ⓐ Ⓑ Ⓒ Ⓓ
113 Ⓐ Ⓑ Ⓒ Ⓓ	138 Ⓐ Ⓑ Ⓒ Ⓓ	163 Ⓐ Ⓑ Ⓒ Ⓓ	188 Ⓐ Ⓑ Ⓒ Ⓓ
114 Ⓐ Ⓑ Ⓒ Ⓓ	139 Ⓐ Ⓑ Ⓒ Ⓓ	164 Ⓐ Ⓑ Ⓒ Ⓓ	189 Ⓐ Ⓑ Ⓒ Ⓓ
115 Ⓐ Ⓑ Ⓒ Ⓓ	140 Ⓐ Ⓑ Ⓒ Ⓓ	165 Ⓐ Ⓑ Ⓒ Ⓓ	190 Ⓐ Ⓑ Ⓒ Ⓓ
116 Ⓐ Ⓑ Ⓒ Ⓓ	141 Ⓐ Ⓑ Ⓒ Ⓓ	166 Ⓐ Ⓑ Ⓒ Ⓓ	191 Ⓐ Ⓑ Ⓒ Ⓓ
117 Ⓐ Ⓑ Ⓒ Ⓓ	142 Ⓐ Ⓑ Ⓒ Ⓓ	167 Ⓐ Ⓑ Ⓒ Ⓓ	192 Ⓐ Ⓑ Ⓒ Ⓓ
118 Ⓐ Ⓑ Ⓒ Ⓓ	143 Ⓐ Ⓑ Ⓒ Ⓓ	168 Ⓐ Ⓑ Ⓒ Ⓓ	193 Ⓐ Ⓑ Ⓒ Ⓓ
119 Ⓐ Ⓑ Ⓒ Ⓓ	144 Ⓐ Ⓑ Ⓒ Ⓓ	169 Ⓐ Ⓑ Ⓒ Ⓓ	194 Ⓐ Ⓑ Ⓒ Ⓓ
120 Ⓐ Ⓑ Ⓒ Ⓓ	145 Ⓐ Ⓑ Ⓒ Ⓓ	170 Ⓐ Ⓑ Ⓒ Ⓓ	195 Ⓐ Ⓑ Ⓒ Ⓓ
121 Ⓐ Ⓑ Ⓒ Ⓓ	146 Ⓐ Ⓑ Ⓒ Ⓓ	171 Ⓐ Ⓑ Ⓒ Ⓓ	196 Ⓐ Ⓑ Ⓒ Ⓓ
122 Ⓐ Ⓑ Ⓒ Ⓓ	147 Ⓐ Ⓑ Ⓒ Ⓓ	172 Ⓐ Ⓑ Ⓒ Ⓓ	197 Ⓐ Ⓑ Ⓒ Ⓓ
123 Ⓐ Ⓑ Ⓒ Ⓓ	148 Ⓐ Ⓑ Ⓒ Ⓓ	173 Ⓐ Ⓑ Ⓒ Ⓓ	198 Ⓐ Ⓑ Ⓒ Ⓓ
124 Ⓐ Ⓑ Ⓒ Ⓓ	149 Ⓐ Ⓑ Ⓒ Ⓓ	174 Ⓐ Ⓑ Ⓒ Ⓓ	199 Ⓐ Ⓑ Ⓒ Ⓓ
125 Ⓐ Ⓑ Ⓒ Ⓓ	150 Ⓐ Ⓑ Ⓒ Ⓓ	175 Ⓐ Ⓑ Ⓒ Ⓓ	200 Ⓐ Ⓑ Ⓒ Ⓓ

TOEIC 分數試算參考表

聽力部分		閱讀部分	
答對題數	換算分數範圍	答對題數	換算分數範圍
96~100	475~495	96~100	455~495
91~95	440~480	91~95	415~460
86~90	415~460	86~90	390~435
81~85	380~430	81~85	360~405
76~80	350~405	76~80	330~380
71~75	320~370	71~75	300~350
66~70	290~340	66~70	270~320
61~65	260~310	61~65	235~280
56~60	240~280	56~60	205~250
51~55	210~260	51~55	175~220
46~50	190~230	46~50	150~190
41~45	165~210	41~45	125~165
36~40	145~185	36~40	105~145
31~35	120~165	31~35	85~125
26~30	100~140	26~30	60~100
21~25	75~120	21~25	45~80
16~20	50~100	16~20	30~65
11~15	30~70	11~15	20~55
6~10	10~50	6~10	15~40
1~5	5~30	1~5	5~20
0	5	0	5

Test 1 分數試算

	答對題數	換算分數範圍
Listening		
Reading		
Total Score		

LISTENING TEST

I 6/6 /-0 0 0 1 2 3   V (101-130) 4/30 -9 -2/6 時間取建議 Reading
II (7-31) 23/25 -6 -6 /2   VI (131-146) 13/16 -3 -1/2 {
III (32-70) 27/39 -12 /10/12   VII (147-200) 45/53 -8 /-5/7 (5 分/60 分
IV (71-100) 22/30 -8 /2/6   76-80 (79) 330~380
Part

678 → 350-405 (76-80) (-)370 + 370 = 740   390+40=790 41 405=87%
(二)

In the Listening test, you are asked to demonstrate how well you understand spoken English. There are four parts to the test and directions are given for each part before it starts. The entire Listening test will last approximately 45 minutes. You must mark your answers on the separate answer sheet. Do not write your answers in your test book.

Part I. ► Photographs

曲目 1

Directions: For each question in this part, you will hear four statements about a picture in your test book. You must select the statement (A), (B), (C), or (D) that best describes the picture, and mark your answer on your answer sheet. The statements will not be printed in your test book and will be spoken only once. Look at the example picture below.

Example

You will hear:
Now listen to the four statements.
(A) The man is <u>checking in.</u> 登記入住
(B) The man is applying for a job.
(C) The woman is not <u>on duty.</u> 執勤.
(D) There are some pictures hanging on the wall.

Statement (A), "The man is checking in." is the best description of the picture, so you should mark answer (A) on your answer sheet. Now, Part One will begin.

1. C ✓

wearing in a casual attire (informal 非正式，輕便服裝)

2. B ✓

operating a photocopier = Xerox machine.

take off
four
closed

3. D ✓

4. A ✓

5. B ✓   making or presentation

6. A ✓   congested traffic 壅塞的

Part II. ► Question-Response 記前懂字)

曲目 2

Directions: You will hear a question or statement and three responses. Select the best response to the question or statement, and mark the letter (A), (B), or (C) on your answer sheet. The responses will not be printed in your test book and will be spoken only once.

Example

You will hear: How are you doing?
You will also hear:
(A) I'm doing okay. How are you?
(B) Oops, my bad.
(C) My company is making profits.

The best response to the question "How are you doing?" is choice (A) "I'm doing okay. How are you?" So (A) is the correct answer. You should mark answer (A) on your answer sheet. Now, Part Two will begin.

I don't know what time is available. / sales rep. (representatives) 業務代表

7. Mark your answer on your answer sheet. B *Goi*

8. Mark your answer on your answer sheet. B

9. Mark your answer on your answer sheet. A

10. Mark your answer on your answer sheet. A
敖 I almost finished. (due)→到期

11. Mark your answer on your answer sheet. C
Just let me send out this

12. Mark your answer on your answer sheet. A
The class ... dismissed 解散

13. Mark your answer on your answer sheet. A
There is no advance anyway

14. Mark your answer on your answer sheet. C
I have to pull an all-nighter tonight / lent you a hand

15. Mark your answer on your answer sheet. A

16. Mark your answer on your answer sheet. B

17. Mark your answer on your answer sheet. C

18. Mark your answer on your answer sheet. C

19. Mark your answer on your answer sheet. A

20. Mark your answer on your answer sheet. A

21. Mark your answer on your answer sheet. B
where→conference room

22. Mark your answer on your answer sheet. A
need one more day to get it done.

23. Mark your answer on your answer sheet. B
work his butt off 認真工作

24. Mark your answer on your answer sheet. A

25. Mark your answer on your answer sheet. A
practice yoga regularly

26. Mark your answer on your answer sheet. B

27. Mark your answer on your answer sheet. C

28. Mark your answer on your answer sheet. A

29. Mark your answer on your answer sheet. B

30. Mark your answer on your answer sheet. C

31. Mark your answer on your answer sheet. A

It's rain outside. So you'd better stay home.

Part III. ► Conversations

曲目 3

Directions: You will hear some conversations. For each conversation, you will be asked to answer three questions about what the speakers say. Select the best response to each question and mark the letter (A), (B), (C), or (D) on your answer sheet. The conversations will not be printed in your test book and will be spoken only once.

32. What is most likely the man's job?
    (A) A hotel employee
    (B) A sales manager
    (C) A conference attendee
    (D) A hotel customer

33. Why does the woman call?
    (A) To reserve a double room
    (B) To make an appointment
    (C) To reserve a meeting venue
    (D) To cancel a reservation

34. What does the woman need the room for?
    (A) Job interview
    (B) Training session
    (C) Marketing meeting
    (D) Technical discussion

35. Where does the conversation most likely take place?
    (A) In a hotel
    (B) In an office
    (C) At an airport
    (D) In Japan

36. What does the woman think of the conference?
    (A) It is a good opportunity to make new friends.
    (B) It is a waste of time.
    (C) It is a perfect way to communicate with clients.
    (D) It is a wonderful opportunity to see old colleagues.

37. What suggestion does the man give to the woman?
    (A) To make a hotel reservation as soon as possible
    (B) To call colleagues in other branches
    (C) To meet old friends more often
    (D) To visit Japan again soon

38. What is most likely the relationship between the two speakers?
    (A) Professor and student
    (B) Vendor and distributor
    (C) Supervisor and subordinate
    (D) CEO and secretary

39. What does the woman think of the man's suggestion?
    (A) She hopes he could reconsider.
    (B) She needs some time to think more thoroughly.
    (C) She thinks the idea is worth discussing further.
    (D) She will consult with her boss first.

40. What will the two speakers probably do next?
(A) Develop new products
(B) Attend a presentation
(C) Sign an agreement
(D) Arrange a further meeting

41. What department do the speakers probably work in?
(A) Administration
(B) Engineering
(C) Marketing
(D) Research & Development

42. What does the man want to know?
(A) What advertising methods are more effective
(B) How the company can make more profits
(C) Where the meeting should be held
(D) Why they can't invest more in advertising

43. What does the woman say about online ads?
(A) Its popularity is growing.
(B) It is old-fashioned.
(C) Customers don't like it.
(D) It will be replaced by other media.

44. What are they talking about?
(A) Marketing activities
(B) Meeting agenda
(C) Ordering processes
(D) Sales strategies

45. Who should approve the order?
(A) The vendor
(B) The supervisor
(C) The accountant
(D) The CFO

46. What action should the accounting department take?
(A) Pay for the order
(B) Keep the invoice in the drawer
(C) Write "goods received" on the invoice
(D) Call the supplier

47. What business is the man most likely in?
(A) Car manufacturing
(B) Consulting
(C) Education
(D) Engineering

48. What information does the man want to know?
(A) New software systems
(B) Job interview strategies
(C) Custom-made communication courses
(D) Company meeting schedules

49. What will the woman most likely do next?
(A) Provide the man a quotation
(B) Transfer the call to a course coordinator
(C) Design a new course
(D) Fax the man an agreement

50. What are the speakers talking about?
(A) A new company policy
(B) A new product
(C) A newly formed team
(D) A new accounting system

51. How does the woman react to the proposal?
(A) She doesn't care that much.
(B) She is all in favor of it.
(C) She thinks it doesn't make any sense.
(D) She hopes her kids really like it.

52. What is most likely the woman's job?
(A) HR director
(B) Janitor
(C) Engineer
(D) Accountant

53. What's the man's problem?
(A) He needs to change his train schedule.
(B) He needs to take sick leave.
(C) He needs to cancel his trip.
(D) He needs to relocate to Stony Brook.

54. Who is most likely the woman?
  (A) The man's student
  (B) The man's assistant
  (C) The man's lawyer
  (D) The man's client

55. When will the man take the train?
  (A) At 10 a.m.
  (B) At 11:30 a.m.
  (C) At 3 p.m.
  (D) At 5 p.m.

56. Why does the man call?
  (A) To ask about a job opening
  (B) To set up an interview
  (C) To file a complaint
  (D) To promote a product

57. What does the woman say about the job?
  (A) It has been filled.
  (B) It is a management level position.
  (C) It requires a lot of traveling.
  (D) It is still open.

58. What will the man most likely do next?
  (A) Fax the woman his application form
  (B) Double check with his friend
  (C) Ask more details about the position
  (D) Go visit the woman's company himself

59. What are the speakers talking about?
  (A) The way to pick up Mr. Smith
  (B) Mr. Smith's travel arrangement
  (C) Linda's performance review
  (D) Stacy's job responsibilities

60. How will Mr. Smith be picked up?
  (A) By a taxi
  (B) By a shuttle bus
  (C) By a limo
  (D) By Stacy

61. What will the woman probably do next?
  (A) Write Mr. Smith an email
  (B) Call Stacy to arrange transportation details
  (C) Drive to the airport to pick up her client
  (D) Cancel the meeting with Ms. Brook

62. Who is most likely the man?
  (A) A truck driver
  (B) A sales representative
  (C) An English teacher
  (D) A dancer

63. Where are most likely the speakers?
  (A) In a restaurant
  (B) At an airport
  (C) In an exhibition center
  (D) At home

64. Please look at the chart. What product is the woman probably not interested in?

Product	Note
Notebooks	Recycled paper
Pens	Eco-certified
Staplers	n/a
Folders	Biodegradable plastic

  (A) Notebooks
  (B) Staplers
  (C) Pens
  (D) Folders

65. What is the woman probably doing?
  (A) Helping a guest to check out
  (B) Giving a lecture
  (C) Playing with kids
  (D) Presenting a product

66. What is the man's major concern?
    (A) Bad service
    (B) High hotel rate
    (C) Lousy weather condition
    (D) Small room

67. Please look at the table. What type of room did the man most likely live in?

Type of Room	List Price	Discounted Price
Family Fun	US$300	US$280
Standard	US$200	US$185
Ocean View	US$230	US$200
Cozy Suite	US$280	US$250

    (A) Standard
    (B) Ocean View
    (C) Family Fun
    (D) Cozy Suite

68. What is the man doing?
    (A) Opening a baseball game
    (B) Hosting a sales meeting
    (C) Preparing reports for the woman
    (D) Interviewing a job applicant

69. Who is most likely the woman?
    (A) An interviewee
    (B) An English teacher
    (C) An HR specialist
    (D) A Japanese artist

70. Please look at the CV. Where did the woman stay in 2006?

Jenny Lee
Work Experience
2002-2004 Sales Assistant, Best Software Inc., NJ, USA
2005-2007 Specialist, Yamaha Co., Tokyo, Japan
2007-2008 Marketing Coordinator, PSG Corp., Taipei, Taiwan
2008-2015 Designer, Rose Advertising, NY, USA

    (A) Tokyo, Japan
    (B) Taipei, Taiwan
    (C) New York, USA
    (D) New Jersey, USA

Part IV. ► Talks

曲目 4

Directions: You will hear some talks given by a single speaker. For each talk, you will be asked to answer three questions about what the speaker says. Select the best response to each question and mark the letter (A), (B), (C), or (D) on your answer sheet. The talks will not be printed in your test book and will be spoken only once.

71. Who is most likely the speaker?
    (A) A radio program host
    (B) A local company owner
    (C) A university professor
    (D) Mr. Oliver Jenkins

72. Who is Mr. Oliver Jenkins?
    (A) A factory worker
    (B) A director of a cookie company
    (C) A weather forecaster
    (D) A civil servant

73. Besides managing a company, what else is Mr. Jenkins concerned about?
    (A) The climate change issue
    (B) The radio program quality
    (C) The compulsory education
    (D) The welfare of employees

74. Why can't Mr. Nolan arrive in Taipei on time?
    (A) Because of the bad weather condition
    (B) Because he missed his flight
    (C) Because he canceled the trip
    (D) Because he doesn't know which hotel he will stay

75. When will Mr. Nolan arrive in Taipei?
    (A) Wednesday, the 20th at 11 a.m.
    (B) Tuesday, the 19th at 4 p.m.
    (C) Monday, the 18th at 10 a.m.
    (D) Friday, the 15th at 3 p.m.

76. What will the woman probably do next?
    (A) Fax Mr. Nolan's meeting agenda to the man
    (B) Call the hotel to reschedule room reservation
    (C) Cancel the restaurant reservation
    (D) Reschedule the meeting and inform the others

77. What's the purpose of the conference?
    (A) To talk about marketing approaches
    (B) To recruit more employees
    (C) To plan a company trip
    (D) To sell new books

78. What will be a marketing focus in 2018?
    (A) Online social media
    (B) TV commercial
    (C) Advertising
    (D) Online banners

79. Besides teaching at university, what else does Ms. Legg do?
    (A) Sell advertising
    (B) Work as a part-time consultant
    (C) Write books
    (D) Write blog articles

80. According to the speaker, how is the company doing?
    (A) It's weak.
    (B) It's doing a roaring trade.
    (C) It's in the red this year.
    (D) As good as last year's performance.

81. How does the speaker predict the company performance for next year?
    (A) Continue to rise
    (B) Start to decline
    (C) Drop by 15%
    (D) Boost by 50%

82. What does the speaker say about the customer satisfaction rate?
    (A) It declines by 25%.
    (B) It increases by 15%.
    (C) It remains unchanged.
    (D) It reaches its record low.

83. What is this talk about?
    (A) Environmental issues
    (B) Outdoor events
    (C) Weather forecast
    (D) Traffic condition

84. What will the weather be like tomorrow?
    (A) It will be raining.
    (B) It will be clear.
    (C) It will be cloudy.
    (D) It will be humid.

85. What will happen on Friday?
    (A) The temperature will drop below zero.
    (B) There will be a lot of snow.
    (C) There will be light scattered showers.
    (D) The weather will be hot and sunny.

86. What is the purpose of this announcement?
    (A) To invite passengers to board the plane
    (B) To announce a delayed departure information
    (C) To invite passengers to board the train
    (D) To inform passengers of a gate change

87. Who is invited to board the plane first?
    (A) Passengers flying to Taipei
    (B) Passengers with credit cards
    (C) Passengers with large suitcases
    (D) Passengers with small children

88. When will the regular boarding begin?
    (A) In 10 minutes
    (B) In 20 minutes
    (C) In 30 minutes
    (D) In 40 minutes

89. What's the problem with the train services?
    (A) They have been delayed by 30 minutes.
    (B) The platform is undergoing renovation.
    (C) All train tickets are sold out.
    (D) Train conductors are on strike.

90. What time did the signaling problem happen?
    (A) 10 a.m.
    (B) 2 p.m.
    (C) 2:30 p.m.
    (D) 10:30 a.m.

91. What are engineers doing now?
    (A) Fixing problems
    (B) Going on vacations
    (C) Selling train tickets
    (D) Apologizing to passengers

92. What kind of product is Winnie Chen selling?
    (A) Snacks
    (B) Jeans
    (C) Books
    (D) Interior design

93. Who is most likely Ms. Kelly Hung?
    (A) A fashion designer
    (B) A doctor
    (C) A shoe vendor
    (D) An event planner

94. What is Ms. Hung asked to do next?
    (A) Fax Winnie the design draft
    (B) Email Winnie the contract
    (C) Call Winnie back to discuss details
    (D) Look for Winnie's number in the White Pages

95. Who is most likely the speaker?
    (A) An interior designer
    (B) A hotel guest
    (C) A hotel customer manager
    (D) A business manager

96. Please look at the table. Which hotel is also the work of Good-Deed Hotel's designer?

5-Star Hotel	Designer
Venus Hotel	Tom Walker
Grand Central Inn	James Williams
Hotel Grace	Grace Bush
Great View Resort	Paul Parker

   (A) Grand Central Inn
   (B) Great View Resort
   (C) Hotel Grace
   (D) Venus Hotel

97. What's Mr. Parker's design style?
    (A) Crowded and dark
    (B) Spacious and elegant
    (C) Expensive and luxurious
    (D) Simple and modern

98. Where does the announcement most likely appear?
    (A) On a telephone answering machine
    (B) In a radio program
    (C) In a weather forecast
    (D) In an electronics store

99. Please look at the table. When does the listener probably hear this message?

Day	Time
Monday – Friday	9 a.m. – 6 p.m.
Saturday	10 a.m. – 2 p.m.
Sunday	Closed

   (A) Tuesday 4 p.m.
   (B) Saturday 12 noon
   (C) Friday 5 p.m.
   (D) Saturday 9 a.m.

100. What should the person who wants to make an appointment do?
     (A) Call again tomorrow
     (B) Dial 4373 and leave a message
     (C) Wait for the tone
     (D) Press the pound key

In the Reading test, you are asked to demonstrate how well you understand written English. There are three parts to the test and directions are given for each part before it starts. The entire Reading test will last 75 minutes. You are encouraged to answer as many questions as possible within the time allowed. You must mark your answers on the separate answer sheet. Do not write your answers in your test book.

Part V. ► Incomplete Sentences

Directions: In this part, you will read several single sentences. For each sentence, a word or phrase is missing, and four answer choices are given. Select the best answer to complete the sentence, and mark the letter (A), (B), (C), or (D) on your answer sheet.

101. Production applications are at the foundation of all processes _____ with doing business.
    (A) associated
    (B) association
    (C) associating
    (D) associate

102. A presenter can reasonably assume that the audience arrives with a desire to know _____ the presenter is going to tell them.
    (A) why
    (B) which
    (C) what
    (D) that

103. Organizations today _____ challenged with the implementation of cost effective information security solutions.
    (A) are
    (B) were
    (C) will
    (D) being

104. We have been responsible _____ the ongoing support of Information Technology for over ten years.
    (A) of
    (B) for
    (C) at
    (D) in

105. Just as the speaker said, "A presentation is an exercise in _____."
    (A) persuaded
    (B) persuasive
    (C) persuade
    (D) persuasion

106. Creative people see _____ as creative and give themselves the freedom to create.
    (A) them
    (B) themselves
    (C) their
    (D) they

107. Brainstorming provides a freewheeling environment _____ everyone is encouraged to participate and contribute good ideas.
(A) In that
(B) who
(C) in which
(D) when

108. _____ I brainstorm on my own, I usually tend to produce a wider range of good ideas.
(A) Because
(B) When
(C) Only
(D) If

109. ITCO provides a cost _____ solution for delivering risk management and knowledge management.
(A) effect
(B) efficiency
(C) effective
(D) effectively

110. I ask for your opinion _____ I am investigating the different partnership options we can have in place.
(A) however
(B) because
(C) only if
(D) although

111. This is to inform you that the contract _____ received and I have sent it to the manager for final approval.
(A) has had
(B) has being
(C) have been
(D) has been

112. A one-year free license for internal use can be _____ to partners only after they started to sell the solutions.
(A) provided
(B) provides
(C) provider
(D) providing

113. When individual group members get stuck on an idea, _____ member's creativity and experience can take the idea to the next stage.
(A) each other
(B) another
(C) others
(D) the other

114. You will be _____ receiving an email with the details to log into our Sales portal.
(A) shorten
(B) short
(C) shortly
(D) short of

115. The chair should make it clear that the _____ of the meeting is to generate as many ideas as possible.
(A) objective
(B) objection
(C) objects
(D) objected

116. Royal Network, the region's leading media network, is _____ exceptional candidates to join our Corporate Development Team.
(A) seeking
(B) looking
(C) searching
(D) asking

117. We need to sign an agreement with you _____ proceeding further, clarifying intentions and vision on both sides.
(A) before
(B) since
(C) when
(D) once

118. The chairman should ask people to give their ideas during a meeting, making sure to give everyone a fair opportunity to _____.
(A) contributing
(B) contribution
(C) contribute
(D) contributor

119. Nowadays businesses are faced with the _____ of analyzing a growing landslide of data flowing into their organizations.
(A) integration
(B) challenge
(C) damage
(D) deployment

120. Unlike traditional email systems, Cloud-Mail _____ full advantage of cloud technology, which makes Could-Mail unique in the market.
(A) gets
(B) does
(C) makes
(D) takes

121. With our risk management solution, you can eliminate surprises by identifying risks before _____ become problems.
(A) they
(B) their
(C) theirs
(D) them

122. You are cordially invited to _____ a Rosman MBA Class on March 18th at 6:30 p.m. at our downtown Toronto campus.
(A) guarantee
(B) sample
(C) register
(D) request

123. In today's _____ environment, reputation risk is the number one risk factor organizations face.
(A) competent
(B) compete
(C) competition
(D) competitive

124. Thanks to the increasing _____ of modern life, people have more opportunities to travel abroad.
(A) affluence
(B) affluent
(C) affluently
(D) afflux

125. I wanted to let you know that your email was well-received this morning, _____ as I am leaving for Japan later today, I won't have time to reply for another two days or so.
(A) or
(B) but
(C) therefore
(D) if

126. This is your chance to experience first-hand _____ it is like to be a student at Singapore's top business school.
(A) where
(B) in which
(C) what
(D) why

127. Would you be willing to provide any advice about how I can raise _____ in the Sales Department?
(A) expense
(B) thought
(C) morale
(D) innovation

128. _____ can overseas travel broaden our views, but it can also provide us with an opportunity to experience foreign cultures.
(A) Not only
(B) Furthermore
(C) However
(D) In addition

129. Thank you for your email of October 21st telling us _____ the unfortunate remark made by one of our sales reps.
(A) on
(B) in
(C) of
(D) about

130. While many schools offer scholarships, for most students, business school is a _____ financial investment.
(A) heavy
(B) significant
(C) configurable
(D) valuable

建議時間
前15mm /60mm

Part VI. ► Text Completion

Directions: Read the texts that follow. A word or phrase is missing in some of the sentences. Four answer choices are given below each of these sentences. Select the best answer to complete the text. Then mark the letter (A), (B), (C), or (D) on your answer sheet.

Questions 131 - 134 refer to the following article.

China differs from Taiwan because China is not a democracy.

Many business leaders realize that _____ oneself from the competition is one of the persistent
131. (A) differentiating *(A differentiating)*
     (B) scheduling
     (C) trapping
     (D) satisfying

challenges in the business. Nothing works quite as well as having superior answers to
_____ the customers' needs.
132. (A) respond
     (B) meet
     (C) answer
     (D) reply

_____ even when one can achieve product superiority there remains the problem in service
133. (A) While
     (B) Furthermore
     (C) If
     (D) However

businesses of making sure that the difference _____ recognized and applauded.
134. (A) were
     (B) is
     (C) are
     (D) be

People have difficulty differentiating China and Taiwan.（主观割舍区分）

Although they're not perfect, I can still learn from them.

Questions 135 - 138 refer to the following article.

A resume is the most important job-search _____ by far.
135. (A) letter
(B) sheet
(C) paper
(D) document

Your resume presents and introduces your most significant experiences, skills, _____ academic
136. (A) but
(B) also
(C) and
(D) or

training to potential employers.

Your resume usually meets interviewers before you do, so it's the first _____ an interviewer gets
137. (A) impression
(B) impressive
(C) impress
(D) impressible

of you.

Your resume serves as your personal advertisement. It can be a good tool to get you an interview
opportunity. _____, you should identify your major selling points in your resume.
138. (A) However
(B) Besides
(C) Therefore
(D) If

Questions 139 - 142 refer to the following notice.

If you are attending the Professional Secretary Meeting in Tokyo, Japan, please join Reality experts for informal discussions _____ the future direction of Reality Inc.

139. (A) about
(B) refer
(C) whether
(D) from

What: Open House
When: Tuesday, February 26 – between 9 a.m. and 11 a.m. (come by anytime)
Where: Reality Inc. suite (for _____ location, stop by booth #333)

140. (A) concise
(B) correct
(C) prefect
(D) exact

Come early to get the best size selection of our newest T-shirt!

Refreshments will be _____ throughout the morning.

141. (A) serving
(B) served
(C) serves
(D) serve

Please let us know if you plan to attend by signing up here: www.reality.com/meeting.

We will notify you with the exact location. If you can't make it to the open house, please visit us in the exhibit hall booth #333.

We look forward to _____ you in Tokyo.

142. (A) sees
(B) seeing
(C) saw
(D) see

Questions 143 - 146 refer to the following article.

Nowadays, one way technology influences global cultures is _____ media globalization.

143. (A) thought
(B) through
(C) thorough
(D) though

With the advent of the Internet, people in different parts of the world have been seamlessly connected. Since the 1990s, an increasing amount of Korean pop cultural contents including Korean dramas, songs and celebrities have _____ immense popularity across most Asian countries.

144. (A) gains
(B) gain
(C) gaining
(D) gained

Young people are able to share schedules of Korean concerts and movies, news of Korean celebrities _____ all related information about Korea on the Internet.

145. (A) of
(B) but
(C) and
(D) as

Some people in the U.S. even form a Korean POP fan page on the Facebook that allows people from different countries to share their favorite Korean stars. Thus, we can clearly see that the Internet and media do have a huge _____ on culture distribution in the world.

146. (A) application
(B) impact
(C) setback
(D) difference

Part VII. ► Reading Comprehension

Directions: In this part you will read a selection of texts, such as magazine and newspaper articles, letters, and advertisements. Each text is followed by several questions. Select the best answer for each question and mark the letter (A), (B), (C), or (D) on your answer sheet.

Questions 147 - 148 refer to the following letter.

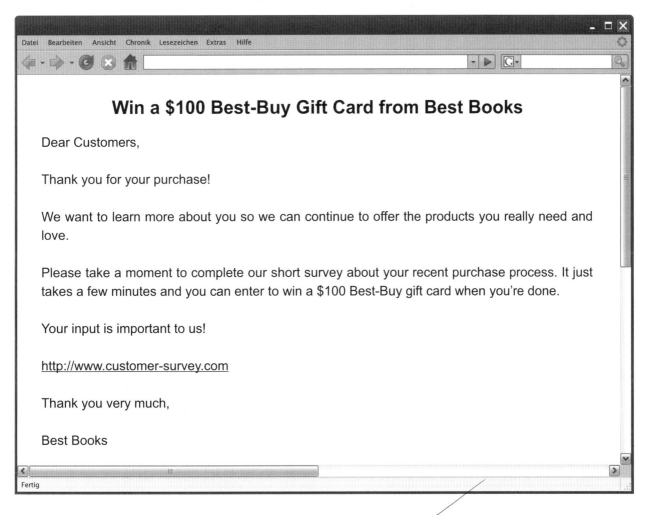

Win a $100 Best-Buy Gift Card from Best Books

Dear Customers,

Thank you for your purchase!

We want to learn more about you so we can continue to offer the products you really need and love.

Please take a moment to complete our short survey about your recent purchase process. It just takes a few minutes and you can enter to win a $100 Best-Buy gift card when you're done.

Your input is important to us!

http://www.customer-survey.com

Thank you very much,

Best Books

147. What's the purpose of this email message?
(A) To get customers' feedback
(B) To propose solutions
(C) To schedule an appointment
(D) To recruit new employees

148. What are customers asked to do?
(A) Purchase more books
(B) Provide opinions online
(C) Enter a contest
(D) Check the latest prices online

Questions 149 - 151 refer to the following advertisement.

Account Managers Wanted

Work Location: Manila

In their role, Associate Managers and Managers lead client engagements to help make better, faster data driven decisions. They apply first-principles-based thinking to solve business problems.

Job Responsibilities:
- Catch up with onsite counterparts to understand client requirements
- Synthesize the information from the call with onsite and help your team make sense of it
- Decide the approach while thinking through possible deadlocks in advance
- Meet up with team members to understand their problems / concerns and to enthuse them in general. We have an open work culture and encourage sharing of ideas.

Requirements:
- Ability to make sense of ambiguity: To lead your team out of murky waters and keep the spirits high in the process
- We like people who believe that they have the ability to influence other people and processes, to mold the environment in a way that helps achieve the team's goals.
- Ability to apply first principles and structured approaches to problem solving as opposed to relying excessively on past domain expertise alone
- An open mind and pleasing personality with good comfort level in interacting and motivating people from diverse backgrounds

Benefits:
- One of the most challenging and diverse work environments where "learning" is a way of life
- Top-notch peer group which will force you to expand your envelope of capabilities
- An open culture where counterparts are encouraged and the emphasis is on collaborative learning

Experience: 3+ years
Educational Qualifications: Bachelors in Engineering / Business Administration / Statistics / Economics

Send cover letter and CV to jobs.singapore@systemtech.com.

149. Where will the employees who are hired for the advertised positions work?
  (A) The Philippines
  (B) Singapore
  (C) Malaysia
  (D) Thailand

150. What job responsibility is mentioned in the advertisement?
  (A) Have a meeting with the CEO once a week
  (B) Make decisions all alone
  (C) Talk to colleagues openly about their concerns
  (D) Ignore customers' requirements

151. What benefit is NOT mentioned in the advertisement?
  (A) Keep learning while working
  (B) Work with brilliant colleagues
  (C) Opportunity to realize your own potential
  (D) Paid training programs

Questions 152 - 153 refer to the following online messages.

Jessie 10:20 a.m.
Hey, Jack. What are you working on? [1]

Jack Lin 10:21 a.m.
Hi, Jessie. [2] Well, I'm working on my presentation slides for the sales meeting this Friday. I'm actually a bit behind.

Jessie 10:22 a.m.
Oh, in that case I don't want to bother you. Well, the thing is that I thought you could give me a hand on my sales report. [3]

Jack Lin 10:24 a.m.
Sure, I'd love to help. You know, as I'm preparing for my sales presentation, I've got pretty good ideas on how to increase our sales revenue. I'd be happy to share my thoughts with you.

Jessie 10:27 a.m.
That would be wonderful, Jack. All right, then how about we meet over lunch and discuss some more details.

Jack Lin 10:28 a.m.
Of course. Then I'll see you at the Cedar Café downstairs at 12:30 p.m.! [4]

152. What does Jessie ask Jack to do?
(A) Buy her some lunch
(B) Help with her sales report
(C) Finish his slides as soon as possible
(D) Attend the meeting on time

153. In which of the positions marked [1], [2], [3], and [4] does the following sentence best belong?
"I really need to come up with effective sales strategies to include in my report."
(A) [1]
(B) [2]
(C) [3]
(D) [4]

Questions 154 - 156 refer to the following article.

The merger of Far-Asian Airlines and Eastern Airways will be announced tomorrow, December 13th. The details of the merger agreement have been worked out and the two airlines' Boards of Directors have approved the deal on Monday evening. After the two carriers merge, they are expected to retain the Far-Asian Airlines name, and the new airline would become the largest air carrier in Asia.

For travelers, nothing will change immediately. These complicated mergers can take averagely more than a year to accomplish, so for travelers nothing will change immediately. But some people express their concern, "Will this eventually mean higher fares for travelers?" Some analysts believe fares won't be greatly impacted, because these two carriers don't compete now on many of their routes. And travelers won't need to worry about their frequent flyer miles either, as the airlines will merge their frequent flyer programs.

One big hurdle for the two airlines to jump, though, is consolidating employees and employee contracts. In this case, agreements have already been worked out with pilots, flight attendants and mechanics, which will help ensure smoother sailing as the airlines combine.

154. What is the purpose of this article?
(A) To announce the merger of two airlines
(B) To inform passengers of changed gates
(C) To describe renovation details at an airport
(D) To attract foreign investment

155. How long will the merger take?
(A) More than a decade
(B) Several years
(C) More than a year
(D) Less than a year

156. What might be the potential problem for the merged airlines?
(A) Combining crew members of two airlines
(B) Dealing with customer complaints
(C) Integrating computer systems
(D) Planning more air routes

BEST Management Trainings

OBJECTIVES →目標

- Improve your sales and marketing management skills: the basics for success
- Build a solid foundation of sales management knowledge, techniques, and tools in this hands-on workshop that covers the entire sales life cycle

OVERVIEW

As the business world grows more competitive, organizations find it necessary to take on an increasing number of sales projects. In this training, you will learn and practice the critical tools and techniques that have been proven necessary for sales management success. This course is specifically designed to focus on the practical application of concepts. You'll return to work with the knowledge and tools you need to get your sales projects started right and completed successfully.

FEES

- 3 days – $2,999 Non Members
- 3 days – $1,999 BEST Training Members
- 3 days – $999 Partners

SCHEDULE		
Date	**Location**	**Duration**
Mar 8, 2017 – Mar 10, 2017	Tokyo, Japan	3 Days
Mar 11, 2017 – Mar 13, 2017	Seoul, Korea	3 Days
Mar 14, 2017 – Mar 16, 2017	Taipei, Taiwan	3 Days
Mar 17, 2017 – Mar 19, 2017	Hong Kong, China	3 Days
Mar 20, 2017 – Mar 22, 2017	Perth, Australia	3 Days
Mar 23, 2017 – Mar 25, 2017	Barcelona, Spain	3 Days
Mar 26, 2017 – Mar 28, 2017	New York, USA	3 Days
Apr 1, 2017 – Apr 3, 2017	Toronto, Canada	3 Days
Apr 4, 2017 – Apr 6, 2017	Chicago, IL, USA	3 Days

REGISTRATION

Please contact Ms. Anna Smith at 1-383-7483-4762 X-122 or visit our website:
http://www.besttrainings.com for more information.

157. What is the main topic of this message?
  (A) Notify employees of a meeting schedule change
  (B) Inform sales and marketing personnel of a training
  (C) Invite managers to attend a conference
  (D) Ask customers to place orders as soon as possible

158. What benefit can a Best Training partner receive?
  (A) A discount
  (B) A free training session
  (C) Some rebate
  (D) A job offer

159. What should a person do if he needs more course information?
  (A) Visit Anna Smith in person
  (B) Visit Best Training website
  (C) Call a toll-free number
  (D) Write Best Training a letter

Questions 160 - 161 refer to the following advertisement. physical fitness 体適能

GO-GYM Fitness Center Membership

GO-GYM Fitness Center is no ordinary gym. Here you're likely to encounter laughter and smiles in a relaxed and comfortable atmosphere. You will also find friendly and helpful fitness instructors who take an active interest in your progress.

關心你的進度

The Fitness Center offers different types of membership schemes to suit your needs.
- GO-GYM Fitness Center Membership
- Healthy Monthly Pass
- Care-free Easy Join

GO-GYM Fitness Center Membership Fees

Type	4 months	8 months	Yearly
Regular	$2,199	$4,099	$8,199
Non-Peak	$1,599	$2,999	$5,999
Basic	$1,299	$2,399	$5,499

GO-GYM Fitness Center Business Hours

Operation Hour	Regular / Basic	Non-Peak
Monday – Friday	6 a.m. – 11 p.m.	8 a.m. – 5 p.m.
Weekend & Public Holiday	7 a.m. – 11 p.m.	7 a.m. – 3 p.m.

Facilities
- Gym Room
- Indoor / Outdoor Swimming Pools
- Sauna Rooms
- Yoga Rooms
- Spa Rooms

160. What is the main purpose of this advertisement?
(A) To announce a training schedule
(B) To attract membership application for a gym
(C) To promote a community event
(D) To fund community activities

161. Which facility is NOT included in the gym?
(A) Yoga room
(B) Swimming pool
(C) Cafeteria
(D) Spa room

Questions 162 - 164 refer to the following advertisement.

System Tech Inc. Reseller Partner Program

Good opportunity to expand your solutions and grow your business
The System Tech Reseller Partner Program is designed to support your business growth, help generate new opportunities, increase profitability and close deals more quickly.

Benefits to Partners
- Association with the leading provider and fastest-growing ERP Software Company
- Favorable purchase margins that improve as partners move into advanced tiers
- Opportunity to provide your specialized services around your client's System Tech purchase
- Access to System Tech Partner Resource Center which includes a library of sales and marketing tools
- Free monthly partner education webinars and certification training programs
- Participation in Quarterly Partner Seminars and invitations to exclusive partner-only events
- Company listing on the System Tech Partner website page

For more information, please visit our website at http://www.systemtech.com or call us at 1-204-3728-7493.

162. For whom is this advertisement most likely intended?
(A) Software developers
(B) Potential business partners
(C) Famous university professors
(D) Computer network experts

163. What is NOT mentioned as a benefit to partners?
(A) High profit margins
(B) Opportunities to attend partner events
(C) Free training programs
(D) Free ERP software products

164. What is indicated about the System Tech Inc.?
(A) It's a company selling ERP solutions.
(B) The company provides 24 / 7 technical services.
(C) Some employees will be laid off soon.
(D) They have branches around the world.

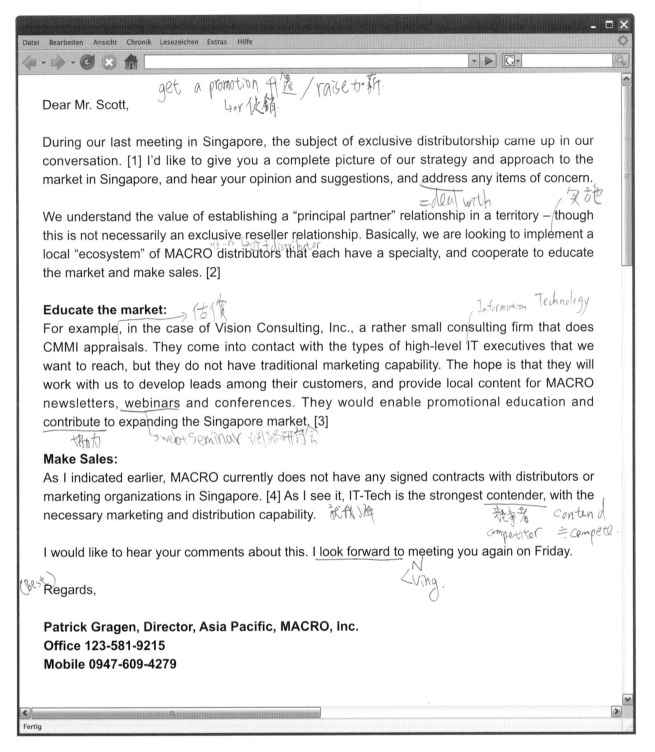

Dear Mr. Scott,

During our last meeting in Singapore, the subject of exclusive distributorship came up in our conversation. [1] I'd like to give you a complete picture of our strategy and approach to the market in Singapore, and hear your opinion and suggestions, and address any items of concern.

We understand the value of establishing a "principal partner" relationship in a territory – though this is not necessarily an exclusive reseller relationship. Basically, we are looking to implement a local "ecosystem" of MACRO distributors that each have a specialty, and cooperate to educate the market and make sales. [2]

Educate the market:
For example, in the case of Vision Consulting, Inc., a rather small consulting firm that does CMMI appraisals. They come into contact with the types of high-level IT executives that we want to reach, but they do not have traditional marketing capability. The hope is that they will work with us to develop leads among their customers, and provide local content for MACRO newsletters, webinars and conferences. They would enable promotional education and contribute to expanding the Singapore market. [3]

Make Sales:
As I indicated earlier, MACRO currently does not have any signed contracts with distributors or marketing organizations in Singapore. [4] As I see it, IT-Tech is the strongest contender, with the necessary marketing and distribution capability.

I would like to hear your comments about this. I look forward to meeting you again on Friday.

Regards,

Patrick Gragen, Director, Asia Pacific, MACRO, Inc.
Office 123-581-9215
Mobile 0947-609-4279

165. What is the purpose of this letter?
    (A) To clarify some partnership details
    (B) To explain some communication techniques
    (C) To recruit some new employees
    (D) To enroll for a training class

166. What is indicated in the letter about Vision
    Consulting?
    (A) They are good at organizing international
        conferences.
    (B) They are not familiar with marketing
        approaches.
    (C) They are the only distributor in Singapore.
    (D) They will meet with Patrick Gragen on
        Friday.

167. In which of the positions marked [1], [2], [3],
    and [4] does the following sentence best
    belong?
    "I want to follow up on this subject further."
    (A) [1]
    (B) [2]
    (C) [3]
    (D) [4]

Questions 168 - 171 refer to the following advertisement.

Best-Ever Restaurant

Location	Sun-City Grand Hotel
	180 Spring Street, Pattaya, Thailand
Opening Hours	Daily 5:30 p.m. – 10:30 p.m.
Bookings	Call 123-363-7030 or book online at www.best-ever.com
Dress Code	A high standard of dress is politely requested
Parking	Complimentary valet parking is available for Best-Ever guests at Sun-City Grand Hotel on the day of dining.

$170 per person

Package includes:
- Your choice of a full one-hour treatment: a signature massage or a signature facial or a warm milk and sandalwood pedicure or a warm milk and sandalwood manicure
- Two-course dinner of Best-Ever's unique blend of Asian, Pacific and traditional European cuisine (choose either an entrée and main or main and dessert from the set menu)
- Complimentary valet car parking at the Sun-City Grand Hotel

Available Monday to Friday, guests must be seated at Best-Ever by 6:30 p.m. Bookings are essential. Call Best Day Spa at 0987-363-7050. Group bookings and gift vouchers are available. Offer is available for a limited time, subject to availability. Package must be redeemed in full on the same day.

168. Where is the Best-Ever Restaurant located?
   (A) In Singapore
   (B) In Thailand
   (C) In China
   (D) In Japan

169. What is NOT true about the dress code?
   (A) Flip-flops are allowed.
   (B) Business suits are allowed.
   (C) Evening gowns are allowed.
   (D) Formal dresses are allowed.

170. How much would a group of four people cost?
   (A) $680
   (B) $860
   (C) $570
   (D) $340

171. Which of the following is true?
   (A) The offer is valid during weekdays.
   (B) Guests can go without a reservation.
   (C) The voucher is good for two years.
   (D) There is no parking space available.

aquire the language more easily.

Questions 172 - 175 refer to the following letter.

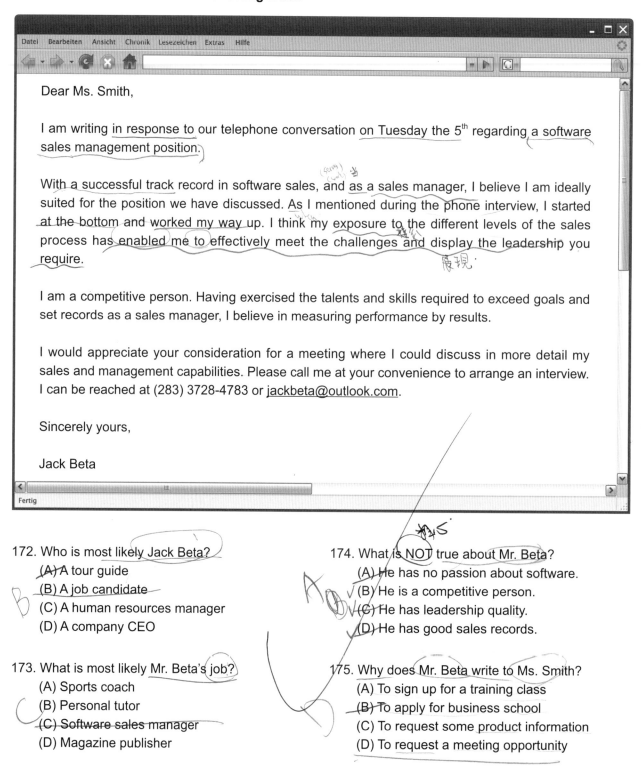

Dear Ms. Smith,

I am writing in response to our telephone conversation on Tuesday the 5th regarding a software sales management position.

With a successful track record in software sales, and as a sales manager, I believe I am ideally suited for the position we have discussed. As I mentioned during the phone interview, I started at the bottom and worked my way up. I think my exposure to the different levels of the sales process has enabled me to effectively meet the challenges and display the leadership you require.

I am a competitive person. Having exercised the talents and skills required to exceed goals and set records as a sales manager, I believe in measuring performance by results.

I would appreciate your consideration for a meeting where I could discuss in more detail my sales and management capabilities. Please call me at your convenience to arrange an interview. I can be reached at (283) 3728-4783 or jackbeta@outlook.com.

Sincerely yours,

Jack Beta

172. Who is most likely Jack Beta?
(A) A tour guide
(B) A job candidate
(C) A human resources manager
(D) A company CEO

173. What is most likely Mr. Beta's job?
(A) Sports coach
(B) Personal tutor
(C) Software sales manager
(D) Magazine publisher

174. What is NOT true about Mr. Beta?
(A) He has no passion about software.
(B) He is a competitive person.
(C) He has leadership quality.
(D) He has good sales records.

175. Why does Mr. Beta write to Ms. Smith?
(A) To sign up for a training class
(B) To apply for business school
(C) To request some product information
(D) To request a meeting opportunity

BIG TREE LODGE RESERVATION FORM

旅店；客棧

PLEASE RETURN THIS FORM DIRECTLY TO THE LODGE
FAX: Reservations (123) 886-2902
Or call: (123) 886-1234 or 1-800-BIGTREE
Or visit www.BIG-TREE.com

Name _____
Address _____
City _____ State _____ ZIP _____ Country _____
Phone (Home) _____ (Office) _____
(Fax) _____ E-mail Address _____

ARRIVAL   Date / Time / Airlines /Flight #   _____ / _____ / _____ / _____
DEPARTURE   Date / Time / Airlines /Flight #   _____ / _____ / _____ / _____

ACCOMMODATIONS
nights at lodge _____
$149 / night: Garden / Golf / Mountain View _____
$169 / night: Partial View _____
$199 / night: Deluxe View _____

• Single or double occupancy
• Additional person $35. Lodge policy limits 3 adults or 2 adults with 2 children per room.
• Children under 12 are complimentary when accompanied by parent.
  免費

Sharing room with _____
                              Name of individual (If children, please list names & ages)

Special Requests (not guaranteed):
_____ One King OR _____ 2 Double Beds
_____ Smoking OR _____ Non-smoking

GUEST NAME: (Please print) _____

That person is a fashion icon

Location: North Africa
Type of Accommodation: Lodge
Comfort Level: Luxury

OVERVIEW
Big Tree Lodge is a six-suite award-winning luxury hideaway set on the banks of the Rocky River in the exclusive Sugi Private Game Reserve. The iconic lodge offers exceptional views extending onto the open sand banks of the Sugi National Park.

Expect exciting game viewing, or opt for a fascinating bush walk. Game vehicles are equipped with bird books and binoculars, while blankets and hot-water bottles are provided to take the chill out of early morning game drives.

RECENT PRESS
- Situated in a private concession in the exclusive Sugi Private Game Reserve
- Exquisite luxury lodge, small and intimate with a contemporary, modern feel
- Private and tailored service – perfect for honeymooners
- Unbelievably spacious safari villas, each with its own rim-flow pool and butler service
- Enjoy the fantastic spa treatments in the privacy of your suite
- Safari fine dining at its best – expect freshly prepared cuisine

176. What is indicated about the hotel?
(A) It is the cheapest one in the area.
(B) It won some awards before.
(C) It is located in Asia.
(D) It is currently under construction.

177. What activity is NOT available to guests?
(A) Viewing wild animals
(B) Visiting Sugi National Park
(C) Shopping in a mall
(D) Walking in the bush

178. Whom is the "tailored service" designed for?
(A) Business travelers
(B) Corporate executives
(C) Newlyweds
(D) Homemakers

179. What is NOT indicated as a way to contact the hotel?
(A) Telephone
(B) Fax
(C) Website
(D) Email

180. Who might live in this hotel free of charge?
(A) A 73-year-old grandpa
(B) A university professor
(C) A 10-year-old child
(D) A middle-aged mother

Charity Donation Foundation

Tuz-Shan is a home in Mountain Village for children who would otherwise be living on the street in terrible conditions. We need to raise funds for the ten oldest children to continue their education. These children need to make themselves more self-sufficient and employable, so they need three years of vocational training. These children are excellent students and have been trying to work hard for a better life – please help!

The problem

In Mountain Village, almost 50% of the population is unable to read and write, and the problem is even more prevalent among girls, who are often not considered deserving of education. Through education, they will benefit, and the community will benefit, from their ability to support themselves.

Possible Solution

We would like to ask for your assistance. It's our mission to educate them so they can take care of themselves and their community. Most children plan to study for practical vocations like hotel management, nursing and medical technician positions.

Please donate and make a difference today!

PAYMENT METHOD

☐ By Personal Check or ☐ By Company Check or ☐ By Credit Card

Type: ☐ Visa ☐ MasterCard ☐ American Express ☐ Other Card _____

Card Number: _____

Exp. Date: ____ ____ / 20 ____ ____ (Month / Year)

Cardholder's Name: _____
(Please Print)

Signature: _____

Date: _____

We also accept donations by mobile phone and wire transfer.

181. What is the main purpose of the first article?
(A) Ask people to join the foundation's
workforce
(B) Encourage people to donate so children
can receive education
(C) Ask foundation employees to work overtime
during the weekend
(D) Inform customers to pay by their credit
cards

182. What can be inferred from the article about the
Mountain Village?
(A) Most females are illiterate.
(B) People there are good at math.
(C) It has a highly developed transportation
system.
(D) It is a prosperous city.

183. What would most children in the Mountain
Village like to study?
(A) Company regulations
(B) Successful case studies
(C) Deep theories
(D) Practical vocations

184. What is NOT required on the payment form?
(A) Credit card number
(B) Cardholder's name
(C) Type of credit card
(D) Cardholder's birthday

185. What is NOT mentioned as an alternative
donation method?
(A) Wire transfer
(B) Check
(C) Mobile device
(D) Cash

Questions 186 - 190 refer to the following advertisement, form, and letter.

Your Rich Bank VISA Card and ATM Card

If you want the flexibility to purchase whatever you need and a card that is safe and secure,
then the Rich Bank Visa Card is the perfect solution for you.

- Your Visa Card is fast! Present your card at time of purchase, sign the receipt and you're on
your way.
- You get a receipt with every purchase and a detailed record of every transaction on your
account statement.
- Make purchases from merchants anywhere and get cash out of your personal or business
checking and savings accounts at ATMs worldwide.
- Your Visa Card is safer than carrying checks or cash.
- Your Visa Card is accepted in millions of places worldwide and is great for Internet or
telephone purchases.

Apply today by simply filling out the application form.

✳ merchane 商人

RICH BANK VISA CARD

Directions: Complete the form below. After you have finished and signed it, bring it to your nearest Rich Bank location.

Applicant
Name: _____Linda Jones_____
Address: _____229 Cedar Street_____
Address 2 _____
City: _____Teaneck_____
State: _____New Jersey_____
ZIP code: _____47739_____ → 邮递区号
Cell phone: _____573-4388-5882_____
Date of Birth: _____1987_____
Employer: _____Best-Software Company_____

Co-Applicant
Name: _____
Address: _____
Address 2 _____
City: _____
State: _____
ZIP code: _____
Cell phone: _____
Date of Birth: _____
Employer: _____

底隆的人

Signatures: The undersigned agrees the information herein is true and complete. The undersigned authorizes Rich Bank to verify credit and employment history and / or to obtain a credit report from a credit reporting agency.

Applicant's Signature _____Linda Jones_____ Date _____6/4/2018_____
Co-Applicant's Signature _____ Date _____

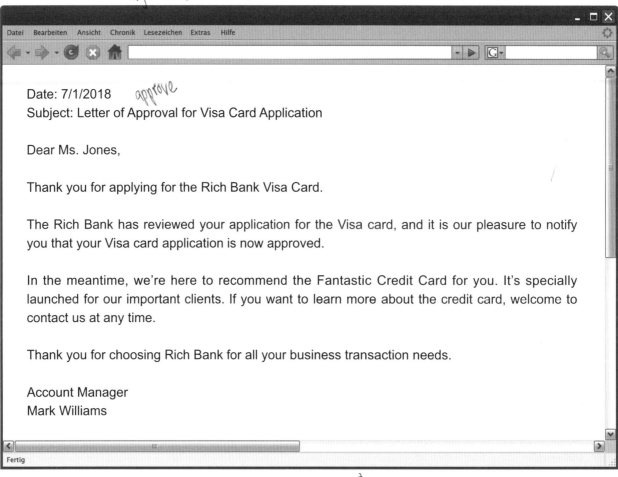

Date: 7/1/2018

Subject: Letter of Approval for Visa Card Application

Dear Ms. Jones,

Thank you for applying for the Rich Bank Visa Card.

The Rich Bank has reviewed your application for the Visa card, and it is our pleasure to notify you that your Visa card application is now approved.

In the meantime, we're here to recommend the Fantastic Credit Card for you. It's specially launched for our important clients. If you want to learn more about the credit card, welcome to contact us at any time.

Thank you for choosing Rich Bank for all your business transaction needs.

Account Manager
Mark Williams

186. What is the purpose of the first message?
(A) Recruit new financial advisors
(B) Announce a merger between two banks
(C) Attract people to apply for Rich Bank's charge cards
(D) Encourage foreign investments

187. What is mentioned about a Rich Bank Visa Card?
(A) It's accepted only in some limited places.
(B) Carrying a Visa card is safer than carrying cash.
(C) The application process is very time-consuming.
(D) It's not used for purchasing products online.

188. What should interested applicants do with the application form?
(A) Complete it and bring it to a Rich Bank branch
(B) Sign it and scan it
(C) Email it to the Rich Bank's main office
(D) Fax it to other relatives

189. In the form, the word "verify" in paragraph 3, line 2, is closest in meaning to
(A) check out
(B) opt to
(C) talk about
(D) wait on

190. What is the main purpose of Mr. Williams' letter?
    (A) To decline Ms. Jones' job application
    (B) To inform Ms. Jones that her credit card application has been approved
    (C) To ask Ms. Jones to provide extra credit history information
    (D) To recruit Ms. Jones to work at the Rich Bank

Questions 191 - 195 refer to the following letter, notice, and testimonial.

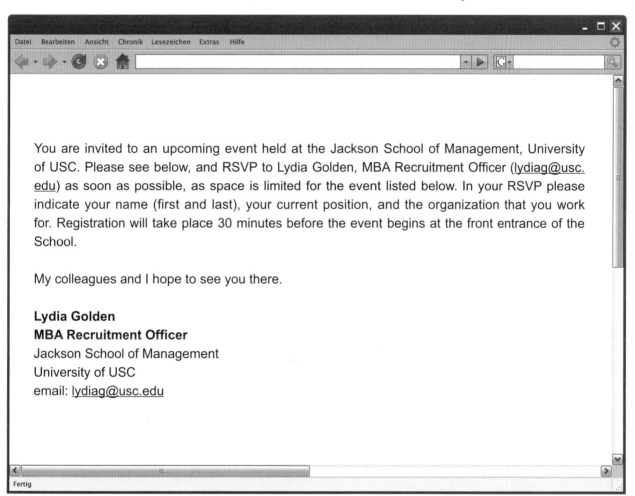

Datei   Bearbeiten   Ansicht   Chronik   Lesezeichen   Extras   Hilfe

You are invited to an upcoming event held at the Jackson School of Management, University of USC. Please see below, and RSVP to Lydia Golden, MBA Recruitment Officer (lydiag@usc.edu) as soon as possible, as space is limited for the event listed below. In your RSVP please indicate your name (first and last), your current position, and the organization that you work for. Registration will take place 30 minutes before the event begins at the front entrance of the School.

My colleagues and I hope to see you there.

Lydia Golden
MBA Recruitment Officer
Jackson School of Management
University of USC
email: lydiag@usc.edu

Fertig

RSCP (Repondez, si'l vous plait.) → 法文

Event Information

March 19th, 4:00 p.m. sharp – 6:00 p.m., Good-Deed Atrium (ground floor), Jackson School of Management, University of USC

All are invited to attend this roundtable presented by our Institute for International Business at Jackson. Dr. Mark Sheehan, Professor and Director of our Jackson International Center for Pension Management, will lead the discussion.

This roundtable is co-sponsored by our Jackson International Center for Pension Management. The session will be hosted by Dr. Jenny Gibson, Professor and Director, Institute of International Business at Jackson.

All are welcome on March 19th. There is no charge to attend. If you have colleagues outside Jackson whom you believe might be interested in the session, please register them as your guests or forward this invitation to them.

Dress code is business casual. Underground parking is available.

PRE-REGISTRATION TO ATTEND ON MARCH 19th IS REQUIRED:
Registration is required to attend. Please email your name, job title and organization name (and the same information about your guests) to: event@usc.edu by 5 p.m. on March 9th. Please note that you will not receive a confirmation of your registration.

Testimonial: Kuan-Chun Chen, Taiwan, 2017

The major reason why I decided to pursue an MBA degree was that I wanted to work full time while pursuing an MBA so that I could apply what I learn in class to my work immediately. I searched for a number of programs and attended their information sessions. I eventually decided on the MBA program at University of USC, because I was fascinated by the high quality of education this university provided. For those who are considering to study MBA further, I would definitely recommend the MBA program of University of USC. Through the program, you will realize that you learn not only from top-notch professors but also by discussing with classmates from various countries and industries. You will also enjoy the moment when you effectively apply what you learn to your real work. Most importantly, the connections with people from University of USC will certainly enhance your future career.

191. What event is being arranged?
(A) A hands-on workshop
(B) A job fair
(C) An MBA information session
(D) A technical meeting

192. What is NOT mentioned as an element when registering for the event?
(A) Position
(B) Name
(C) Organization
(D) Birthday

193. How long will the event last?
(A) 2 hours
(B) 4 hours
(C) 6 hours
(D) 7 hours

194. About the event, which of the following is true?
(A) It's free of charge.
(B) Attendees can pay for the enrollment by cash.
(C) This event is only open to Jackson School students.
(D) The event is usually held in summer.

195. What is true about Kuan-Chun Chen?
(A) He is a professor teaching at University of USC.
(B) He had excellent studying experience at University of USC.
(C) He just graduated from college and has no work experience at all.
(D) He only talked to Taiwanese students when he studied abroad.

Questions 196 - 200 refer to the following letters and comments.

2/8/2018
Mr. Steve Bush
Room: 883

Dear Mr. Bush,

Welcome to Grand Inn. On behalf of all my staff, I hope you and your family will be having a pleasant stay here in Grand Inn.

We look forward to demonstrating services and skills distinctive and special to Grand Inn, which is fully equipped with fine dining, spa, business centers and Health club facilities to cater to our guests. We want to be attentive and sensitive to your needs.

Should you require any additional help or information during your stay with us, please do not hesitate to contact our service staff in the lobby or dial #11 from your room at any time. At your convenience, please provide us with your feedback, comments or even questions as your opinions will be valuable for us.

Once again we would like to take this opportunity to thank you for choosing Grand Inn.

Yours sincerely,
Linda Chen
General Manager
Grand Inn

Guest Comments:

We recently stayed at the Grand Inn and were delighted to stay there for three nights. All staff members were both caring and helpful. We would say they were some of the best service people we have ever encountered. They did whatever they could to make sure all guests had a lovely stay. The hotel itself is conveniently situated and just within walking distance to the famous Water Square. My wife also confirmed what I thought and she felt that Grand Inn is one of the best hotels in Spring City. Without question, we'll definitely return.

Steve Bush, 2/12/2018

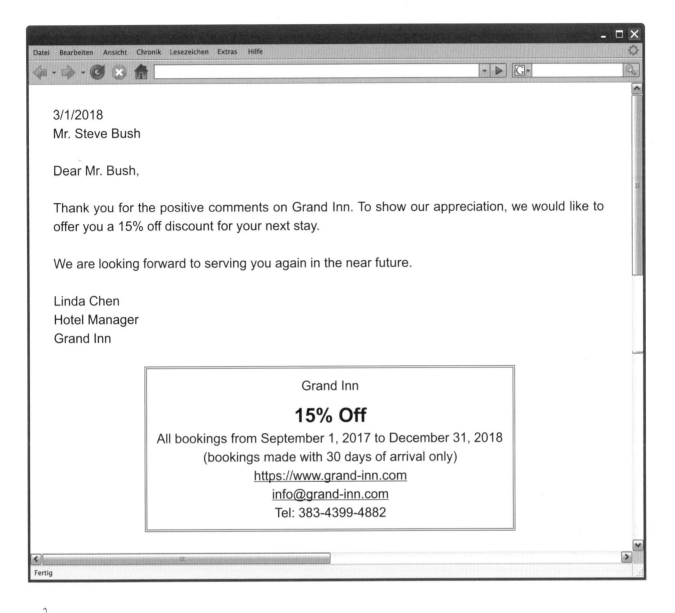

3/1/2018
Mr. Steve Bush

Dear Mr. Bush,

Thank you for the positive comments on Grand Inn. To show our appreciation, we would like to offer you a 15% off discount for your next stay.

We are looking forward to serving you again in the near future.

Linda Chen
Hotel Manager
Grand Inn

Grand Inn

15% Off

All bookings from September 1, 2017 to December 31, 2018
(bookings made with 30 days of arrival only)
https://www.grand-inn.com
info@grand-inn.com
Tel: 383-4399-4882

196. What is the purpose of Linda Chen's first letter to Steve Bush?
(A) To welcome hotel guests
(B) To file a complaint
(C) To invite seminar attendees
(D) To enlist soldiers

197. In Linda's first letter, the word "distinctive" in paragraph 2, line 1, is closest in meaning to
(A) tedious
(B) ordinary
(C) usual
(D) unique

198. What can be inferred about Mr. Steve Bush?
(A) His stay in Grand Inn was for business purposes.
(B) He has been working in Grand Inn for quite a long time.
(C) He is satisfied with the service in Grand Inn.
(D) He is still a single man.

199. What is NOT true about Grand Inn?
(A) It's located in Spring City.
(B) It's one of the oldest hotels in the world.
(C) It has business amenities.
(D) It is near Water Square.

200. According to the coupon, if Mr. Bush reserves a $200 room for a night, how much will he need to pay?

(A) $190

(D) $170

(C) $200

(D) $150

NEW TOEIC

Test 2

In the Listening test, you are asked to demonstrate how well you understand spoken English. There are four parts to the test and directions are given for each part before it starts. The entire Listening test will last approximately 45 minutes. You must mark your answers on the separate answer sheet. Do not write your answers in your test book.

Part I. ▶ Photographs

曲目 5

Directions: For each question in this part, you will hear four statements about a p your test book. You must select the statement (A), (B), (C), or (D) that best describes th e, and mark your answer on your answer sheet. The statements will not be printed in you ok and will be spoken only once. Look at the example picture below.

Example

You will hear:
Now listen to the fou atements.
(A) The man is c' king in.
(B) The man is lying for a job.
(C) The wo is not on duty.
(D) Th some pictures hanging on the wall.

 ement (A), "The man is checking in." is the best description of the picture, so you should mark answer (A) on your answer sheet. Now, Part One will begin.

1.

2.

3.

4.

5.

6.

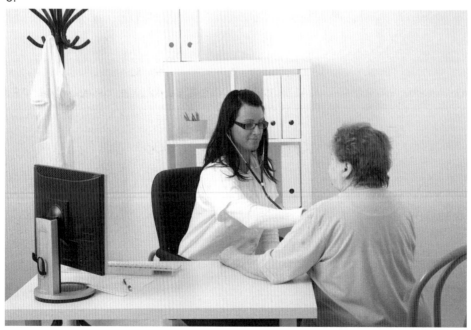

Part II. ► Question-Response

Directions: You will hear a question or statement and three responses. Select the best response to the question or statement, and mark the letter (A), (B), or (C) on your answer sheet. The responses will not be printed in your test book and will be spoken only once.

Example

You will hear: How are you doing?
You will also hear:
(A) I'm doing okay. How are you?
(B) Oops, my bad.
(C) My company is making profits.

The best response to the question "How are you doing?" is choice (A) "I'm doing okay. How are you?" So (A) is the correct answer. You should mark answer (A) on your answer sheet. Now, Part Two will begin.

7. Mark your answer on your answer sheet.

8. Mark your answer on your answer sheet.

9. Mark your answer on your answer sheet.

10. Mark your answer on your answer sheet.

11. Mark your answer on your answer sheet.

12. Mark your answer on your answer sheet.

13. Mark your answer on your answer sheet.

14. Mark your answer on your answer sheet.

15. Mark your answer on your answer sheet.

16. Mark your answer on your answer sheet.

17. Mark your answer on your answer sheet.

18. Mark your answer on your answer sheet.

19. Mark your answer on your answer sheet.

20. Mark your answer on your answer sheet.

21. Mark your answer on your answer sheet.

22. Mark your answer on your answer sheet.

23. Mark your answer on your answer sheet.

24. Mark your answer on your answer sheet.

25. Mark your answer on your answer sheet.

26. Mark your answer on your answer sheet.

27. Mark your answer on your answer sheet.

28. Mark your answer on your answer sheet.

29. Mark your answer on your answer sheet.

30. Mark your answer on your answer sheet.

31. Mark your answer on your answer sheet.

Part III. ► Conversations

Directions. You will hear some conversations. For each conversation, you will be asked to answer three questions about what the speakers say. Select the best response to each question and mark the letter (A), (B), (C), or (D) on your answer sheet. The conversations will not be printed in your test book and will be spoken only once.

32. Why is the man late?
    (A) His car is broken.
    (B) He has difficulty finding the location.
    (C) He misses the train.
    (D) He forgets to bring his GPS.

33. What does the man say about the GPS system?
    (A) He is interested in buying one.
    (B) He thinks it's too expensive.
    (C) He has one already but it's not working.
    (D) He will borrow one from the woman.

34. What does the woman suggest the man do?
    (A) Ask for directions next time
    (B) Bring a map with him
    (C) Purchase a GPS system
    (D) Leave earlier and be on time

35. Who is most likely the woman?
    (A) A customer service manager
    (B) An event host
    (C) A sales manager
    (D) A literature professor

36. Where is the conversation most likely taking place?
    (A) In an office
    (B) In a library
    (C) At an airport
    (D) In a conference room

37. What does the woman suggest doing first when dealing with an upset customer?
    (A) Yell at him
    (B) Listen to him
    (C) Ask him to calm down
    (D) Attend the conference

38. What is the man doing?
    (A) Applying for the driver's license
    (B) Checking the flight schedule
    (C) Signing a contract
    (D) Rescheduling his meeting

39. When will the flight leave?
    (A) 10:30
    (B) 1:35
    (C) 8:37
    (D) 2:30

40. What will the man probably do next?
    (A) Pay by cash
    (B) Cancel the meeting
    (C) Go to Gate 74
    (D) Stay in LA for good

41. What is the man trying to do?
    (A) Buy a van
    (B) Apply for a new credit card
    (C) Rent a car
    (D) Make a hotel reservation

42. What does the woman ask the man to do?
    (A) Complete the form
    (B) Sign an agreement
    (C) Pay a deposit
    (D) Renew the driver's license

43. What does the man need a car for?
    (A) Vacation
    (B) Business
    (C) Pleasure
    (D) Personal issue

44. What are the three speakers talking about?
    (A) Attending a concert on the weekend
    (B) Listening to a radio program
    (C) Inviting Julie to come along
    (D) Finding a new job

45. Why is Gina eager to join her colleagues?
    (A) She has nothing to do on the weekend.
    (B) She has finished the project already.
    (C) She likes Ed Mendoza very much.
    (D) She likes to help others.

46. What does Julie offer to do for Gina?
    (A) Buy her a lunch
    (B) Introduce her to Ed Mendoza
    (C) Provide her with a free ticket
    (D) Help with her project

47. Where is the conversation most likely taking place?
    (A) In an electronics shop
    (B) In a classroom
    (C) In an office
    (D) In a restaurant

48. What is the man's problem?
    (A) He lost the receipt.
    (B) He doesn't know where the switch is.
    (C) His newly purchased radio doesn't work.
    (D) He doesn't know what "AC" means.

49. How long ago did the man buy the radio?
    (A) This morning
    (B) Three weeks ago
    (C) Last week
    (D) Three days ago

50. What are the two speakers talking about?
    (A) A job opening
    (B) A trip to Asia
    (C) A high-paying job
    (D) A telephone interview

51. Where does the man find out about the job?
    (A) In a magazine
    (B) In a newspaper
    (C) On a radio program
    (D) At a job fair

52. What does the woman think of the opportunity?
    (A) It's an easy job.
    (B) The salary is good enough.
    (C) She expects to get a good pay.
    (D) She doesn't want to work abroad.

53. Who is most likely the man?
    (A) A manager
    (B) An engineer
    (C) A secretary
    (D) A janitor

54. What is the woman's problem?
    (A) She lost a case.
    (B) She made some typing mistakes.
    (C) She is leaving the company soon.
    (D) She should have consulted with Grace first.

55. What will the woman probably do next?
    (A) Call Grace's cell phone
    (B) Type the letter over again
    (C) Apologize to Mr. Connie
    (D) Call the client and say sorry

56. Why does the woman make this call?
    (A) To file a complaint
    (B) To place an order
    (C) To apply for a job
    (D) To retrieve her lost item

57. What color is the woman's purse?
    (A) Mauve
    (B) Scarlet
    (C) Brown
    (D) Beige

58. What's written on the woman's purse?
    (A) Her full name
    (B) Her company's name
    (C) Her ID number
    (D) Her initials

59. What is the man impressed with?
    (A) The woman's house
    (B) The woman's office
    (C) The woman's car
    (D) The woman's sales skills

60. Why do Mr. and Mrs. Smith do the house by
    themselves?
    (A) They have a deep pocket.
    (B) They are short of funds.
    (C) They are architects.
    (D) They want to make more money.

61. How does the woman learn cabinetmaking
    skills?
    (A) By attending a vocational school
    (B) By reading books
    (C) By asking her husband
    (D) By listening to radio programs

62. Who is most likely the woman?
    (A) The man's sister
    (B) A hotel manager
    (C) A program designer
    (D) A wedding attendee

63. What is the man planning to do?
    (A) Reserve a table for two people
    (B) Reserve a conference room for a meeting
    (C) Hold a birthday party for his father
    (D) Arrange a company event

64. Look at the table. Which room will the man most
    likely reserve?

Venue	Capacity	Availability
Sunshine Room	35-45 attendees	July, August
Ocean Room	100+ attendees	August, October
Moonlight Room	40 attendees	September
Polar Star Room	50-70 attendees	July, August, September

    (A) Moonlight Room
    (B) Sunshine Room
    (C) Ocean Room
    (D) Polar Star Room

65. Who are most likely the speakers?
    (A) Strangers
    (B) Group members
    (C) Relatives
    (D) Parents

66. What are the speakers discussing?
   (A) Fixing their laptop computers
   (B) Discussing marketing strategies
   (C) Planning a company party
   (D) Choosing a theme for the project

67. Please look at the list. Which website would the speakers like to look at?

1	http://www.waters-save-easy.com
2	http://www.wild-life.net
3	http://www.polar-world.com
4	http://www.eco-products.com

   (A) 4
   (B) 2
   (C) 1
   (D) 3

68. Why is the man calling?
   (A) To invite the woman to a meeting
   (B) To arrange an international conference
   (C) To enquire more about a business event
   (D) To reserve hotel accommodations

69. According to the woman, what's the main theme for the conference?
   (A) Sales and marketing
   (B) Engineering
   (C) Human resources
   (D) Accounting

70. Please look at the table. What discount rate will the man probably receive?

Number of Tickets	Discount Rate
1 ticket	n/a
2-3 tickets	5% off
4-8 tickets	10% off
9+ tickets	15% off

   (A) None
   (B) 10% off
   (C) 5% off
   (D) 15% off

Part IV. ▶ Talks

曲目 8
Directions. You will hear some talks given by a single speaker. For each talk, you will be asked to answer three questions about what the speaker says. Select the best response to each question and mark the letter (A), (B), (C), or (D) on your answer sheet. The talks will not be printed in your test book and will be spoken only once.

71. Who is most likely the man?
(A) A tour guide
(B) A professor
(C) An administrator
(D) An architect

72. What's the speaker's main subject?
(A) A historic city
(B) A great museum building
(C) A famous skyscraper
(D) A beautiful garden

73. What will happen after the speaker's five-minute presentation?
(A) Another two-hour speech
(B) A brief introduction to the city
(C) A question and answer session
(D) An interview with Terrance Legg

74. Where does the announcement probably take place?
(A) At an airport
(B) In a meeting room
(C) At a university
(D) In a restaurant

75. What's the problem with the newly installed system?
(A) Hardware
(B) License
(C) Information flow
(D) Installation

76. What will happen in the coming months?
(A) More training sessions will be arranged.
(B) More staff will be laid off.
(C) More meetings will be held.
(D) More new systems will be installed.

77. Who is the speaker probably talking to?
(A) Students
(B) Sales representatives
(C) Customers
(D) Investors

78. What does the speaker mention about customer complaints?
(A) Its rate decreases.
(B) Its rate increases.
(C) Its rate remains unchanged.
(D) Its rate will fall.

79. What will happen next quarter?
(A) Sales figures will not be good.
(B) More sales training courses will be arranged.
(C) New businesses will be expanded in Asia.
(D) Investors will have more confidence.

80. Who is Mary Fidelity?
(A) An HR director
(B) A new employee
(C) A production manager
(D) An HR specialist

81. What will the people do after lunch?
    (A) Have a meeting with clients
    (B) Have a meeting with the marketing director
    (C) Have a meeting with the production manager
    (D) Have a meeting with the HR specialist

82. Who will most likely speak next?
    (A) The production manager
    (B) The VP of engineering
    (C) The marketing director
    (D) The chief financial officer

83. Where does the speaker probably work?
    (A) In a travel agency
    (B) In the Taipei 101 building
    (C) In a shopping center
    (D) In a night market

84. What is special about the Taipei 101 building?
    (A) It is surrounded by night markets.
    (B) It is one of the tallest buildings in the world.
    (C) It has the largest shopping center inside.
    (D) It is one of the oldest buildings in the world.

85. What will travelers probably do next?
    (A) Go back to the hotel
    (B) Board a plane
    (C) Shop in Taipei 101
    (D) Board a bus

86. Who is most likely the speaker?
    (A) A magazine publisher
    (B) A radio program host
    (C) A city tour guide
    (D) A radio program guest

87. When was the magazine first published?
    (A) In 1980
    (B) In 1897
    (C) In 1998
    (D) In 1889

88. What will probably happen next?
    (A) A tour guide will talk.
    (B) Joan Back will answer questions.
    (C) Ms. Andrea Parker will speak.
    (D) A special guest will sing.

89. What will the weather be like at night?
    (A) Warm and windy
    (B) Hot and windy
    (C) Warm and humid
    (D) Stuffy and rainy

90. What might be the problem overnight?
    (A) High temperature
    (B) Mild wind
    (C) Strong wind
    (D) Heavy rain

91. What time will the next forecast update be?
    (A) 4 p.m.
    (B) 5 p.m.
    (C) 5 a.m.
    (D) 3 p.m.

92. Where does the announcement probably take place?
    (A) In a conference room
    (B) On an airplane
    (C) On a ship
    (D) In an office

93. What time will passengers arrive in Seattle?
    (A) 10 a.m.
    (B) 10 p.m.
    (C) 8 a.m.
    (D) 2 p.m.

94. What will flight attendants do next?
    (A) Ask passengers to fill out forms
    (B) Make another announcement
    (C) Serve beverages
    (D) Fasten seat belts

95. Who is probably the audience of this
   announcement?
   (A) Overseas travelers
   (B) Wellington residents
   (C) Train passengers
   (D) Customer service representatives

96. Where will the train stop?
   (A) It won't stop.
   (B) At platform 2A
   (C) In the information booth
   (D) At platform 3B

97. Please look at the chart. What number should a
   passenger dial if he lost his luggage?

Questions regarding:	Dial extension:
Train Schedules	779
Lost and Found	473
Tickets	398
Wheel Chair Assistance	273

   (A) 473
   (B) 273
   (C) 398
   (D) 779

98. Who is most likely the caller?
   (A) Dr. Dean's sister
   (B) Dr. Dean's assistant
   (C) Dr. Dean himself
   (D) Dr. Dean's patient

99. Please look at the table. On what date will Gary
   Hill most likely meet Dr. Dean?

Date	Time	Dr. Dean's Availability
10/4, Thursday	3 p.m.	Meeting at Boston
10/5, Friday	Whole Day	Meeting at Boston
10/8, Monday	5 p.m.	Jerry Smith
10/9, Tuesday	10 a.m.	Available

   (A) 10/4
   (B) 10/8
   (C) 10/5
   (D) 10/9

100. What is Mr. Gary Hill asked to do next?
   (A) Go to see Dr. Dean tomorrow
   (B) Return Lily's call tomorrow
   (C) Call Dr. Dean next Tuesday
   (D) Email Lily a new schedule

In the Reading test, you are asked to demonstrate how well you understand written English. There are three parts to the test and directions are given for each part before it starts. The entire Reading test will last 75 minutes. You are encouraged to answer as many questions as possible within the time allowed. You must mark your answers on the separate answer sheet. Do not write your answers in your test book.

Part V. ▶ Incomplete Sentences

Directions: In this part, you will read several single sentences. For each sentence, a word or phrase is missing, and four answer choices are given. Select the best answer to complete the sentence, and mark the letter (A), (B), (C), or (D) on your answer sheet.

101. I am pleased to announce that the last quarter's sales figures _____ a record for us.
(A) configure
(B) constitute
(C) combine
(D) combat

102. A third of the employees _____ passed the qualification exam.
(A) have
(B) has
(C) had
(D) had been

103. He works so hard _____ his doctor often tells him to take it easy.
(A) but
(B) then
(C) that
(D) because

104. ITNet is looking for professionals with strategic vision, _____ proven capacity to generate results.
(A) and
(B) or
(C) also
(D) but

105. Where are you considering _____ for vacation?
(A) travels
(B) traveling
(C) traveler
(D) to travel

106. I decided to speak _____ the manager after the presentation.
(A) at
(B) to
(C) about
(D) together

107. Our company offers a competitive _____ and benefits package to our employees.
(A) money
(B) remuneration
(C) loan
(D) penalty

108. People like eating sweet food, _____ chocolate, cake, and other sugar-based items.
(A) such like
(B) such that
(C) such as
(D) such

109. He is such a _____ member of the staff that no one in the company would contradict him.
(A) respective
(B) roopooting
(C) respect
(D) respected

110. We are not attending the conference, _____ a few people from the sales department are.
(A) and
(B) but
(C) so
(D) due to

111. We use _____ huge quantities of pens each month but also oceans of ink.
(A) only
(B) only if
(C) not only
(D) only just

112. You should take a rest. You've kept _____ for 12 hours.
(A) to work
(B) worked
(C) work
(D) working

113. A good sales plan should _____ an executive summary, a customer analysis, and a market forecast.
(A) possess
(B) contain
(C) deliver
(D) exclude

114. We have six team members: one is an assistant, another is a marketing specialist, and _____ are all sales reps.
(A) the others
(B) the other
(C) others
(D) all the other

115. _____ candidates should have excellent leadership skills, and can lead teams from different culture backgrounds.
(A) Interested
(B) Interests
(C) Interesting
(D) Interestingly

116. When the CEO entered the meeting room, everybody _____ talking.
(A) will stop
(B) ended
(C) stopped
(D) stopped to

117. We plan _____ a technical seminar next month.
(A) to arranging
(B) to arrange
(C) arrangement
(D) to have arranged

118. Our goal is to help our clients build a useful system _____ fits each client's unique situation.
(A) when
(B) who
(C) where
(D) that

119. Hawaii has many interesting tropical trees, flowers, _____ beautiful beaches.
(A) and
(B) also
(C) additional
(D) or

120. The best and most direct way for companies to get the right person for the job is to get a _____ from a trusted friend.
(A) reputation
(B) recommendation
(C) resignation
(D) rotation

121. The weather wasn't good yesterday but it's
_____ today.
(A) better
(B) best
(C) goods
(D) worst

122. Business leaders around the world
_____ Mason Business School their
preferred choice for advanced education.
(A) have make
(B) have made
(C) had making
(D) has been making

123. The CEO and his secretary _____ going
to attend that conference.
(A) is
(B) are
(C) will
(D) was

124. Of the two people, one is from China and
_____ is from Japan.
(A) the others
(B) another
(C) others
(D) the other

125. Our Marketing and Sales departments are
working together on a _____ plan for the
new software product.
(A) procedural
(B) promotional
(C) primary
(D) protective

126. The city _____ the conference will be
held is beautiful.
(A) who
(B) in which
(C) what
(D) why

127. Anyone can learn how to operate this machine
_____ he wants to.
(A) since
(B) if
(C) although
(D) but

128. A smile on your face can make a big difference
in your interview success, because it will make
you appear more _____ and confident.
(A) articulate
(B) approachable
(C) strict
(D) diligent

129. Susan didn't get a promotion, _____
disappointed her a lot.
(A) that
(B) what
(C) which
(D) who

130. There are many online price comparison
tools _____ people to get quotes from
different resellers on the Internet today.
(A) used to
(B) available for
(C) popular with
(D) interested in

Part VI. ► Text Completion

Directions: Read the texts that follow. A word or phrase is missing in some of the sentences. Four answer choices are given below each of these sentences. Select the best answer to complete the text. Then mark the letter (A), (B), (C), or (D) on your answer sheet.

Questions 131 - 134 refer to the following article.

In order to help our students fully prepare the university admission, I would like to _____ a few

131. (A) share
(B) lecture
(C) tell
(D) inform

tips on how to put your best foot forward in the interview process.

- **Be yourself.** This sounds obvious, but many applicants get tripped up trying to get inside interviewers' heads. Don't _____ matters further. Tell interviewers about what you care about,

132. (A) standardize
(B) satisfy
(C) complicate
(D) compromise

not what you think interviewers want to hear.

- **Don't ignore your weaknesses.** There's no such thing as a perfect applicant. Everyone has weaknesses. Interviewers will see them, _____ you're better off acknowledging them and

133. (A) in addition
(B) if
(C) but
(D) so

incorporating them into your application instead of hoping interviewers will miss them.

- **Don't stress about grades.** Grades matter. Test scores matter. Essays matter. Everything in the application is important. Do a good job and take everything _____.

134. (A) overwhelmingly
(B) seriously
(C) anxiously
(D) surprisingly

Questions 135 - 138 refer to the following article.

When done properly, a computer network virtualization project can save enterprises money, and it can make company network management far _____, more secure, and more effective.

135. (A) easier
     (B) easy
     (C) easily
     (D) more easily

Please note that the key words here _____ "when done properly".

136. (A) was
     (B) is
     (C) should
     (D) are

Without proper planning, execution, and post-virtualization monitoring, your company's virtualization dream will quickly _____ an expensive nightmare.

137. (A) have become
     (B) become
     (C) became
     (D) becomes

Fortunately, there are steps enterprises can take to _____ a smooth virtualization project.

138. (A) ensure
     (B) manufacture
     (C) happen
     (D) admit

Step 1: Prepare for your company's virtualization well
Step 2: Execute your company's virtualization project fully
Step 3: Manage your company's virtualization infrastructure wisely

Questions 139 - 142 refer to the following article.

Hi, everyone. This is a pretty simple article _____ a very innovative sales technique – leveraging

139. (A) saying
(B) relative
(C) about
(D) around

our customers to sell.

In our class, we'll cover several models about this. One of _____ will be a

140. (A) these
(B) it
(C) him
(D) this

method that combines "online group-coupon" with customer sales. I hope you can ask good questions
to draw out data and ideas that the class can use to propose suggestions.

_____ the process, I will teach some methods for "hypothesis-driven" and "model-driven"

141. (A) When
(B) While
(C) During
(D) At

questioning – which are methods I first learned at Macro Consulting.

I hope you enjoy this exploration of our real-life, innovative case. Perhaps you'll even discover some
excellent suggestions I have not yet _____. I deeply look forward to this, our final session.

142. (A) considers
(B) considering
(C) consideration
(D) considered

Questions 143 - 146 refer to the following article.

In the search for helpful or _____ visual aids, it is all too easy for a presenter to forget the value

143. (A) memories
    (B) memory
    (C) memorized
    (D) memorable

of a small object fished out of the pocket, or a larger one from under the desk. It is worth
_____ that if there is any object, or part of any object, which could be interesting and reasonably

144. (A) noting
    (B) note
    (C) noted
    (D) notes

relevant to display.

For example, a presenter is quite familiar _____ the inside of a smartphone, and he forgets that

145. (A) of
    (B) about
    (C) with
    (D) for

his audience has possibly never _____ one. Simply producing something and holding it up lifts

146. (A) sees
    (B) saw
    (C) seen
    (D) seeing

the presentation for a couple of reasons: 1. It turns an abstract idea into a physical object, and 2. It substitutes a memorable picture for a forgettable word.

新16'15. 剩58'39" (共75mn → 60+15mn)

Part VII. ► Reading Comprehension

Directions: In this part you will read a selection of texts, such as magazine and newspaper articles, letters, and advertisements. Each text is followed by several questions. Select the best answer for each question and mark the letter (A), (B), (C), or (D) on your answer sheet.

Questions 147 - 148 refer to the following memo.

To: Ms. Lorry Anderson
From: Mr. James Legg
Date / Time: November 15th, 2018 / 4 p.m.

Message:
Mr. Legg would like to thank you for a very pleasant and productive visit. He enjoyed seeing all marketing staff and appreciated the time you had together to discuss business opportunities in Hong Kong. And he would also like to thank you for setting up the meetings with the consultants. They were very informative, and he really appreciated it.

He is looking forward to a successful year in 2019. Please always feel free to contact him if there is anything he can do to help with anything you are working on or anything else you would like to discuss.

Message taken by: Sherry Morgan

147. Why did Mr. Legg call Ms. Anderson?
(A) To arrange a visit next month
(B) To reschedule an appointment
(C) To express appreciation
(D) To make a hotel reservation in HK

148. Who is most likely Sherry Morgan?
(A) Ms. Anderson's personal assistant
(B) Mr. Legg's secretary
(C) Ms. Anderson's client
(D) Mr. Legg's accountant

Questions 149 - 151 refer to the following email.

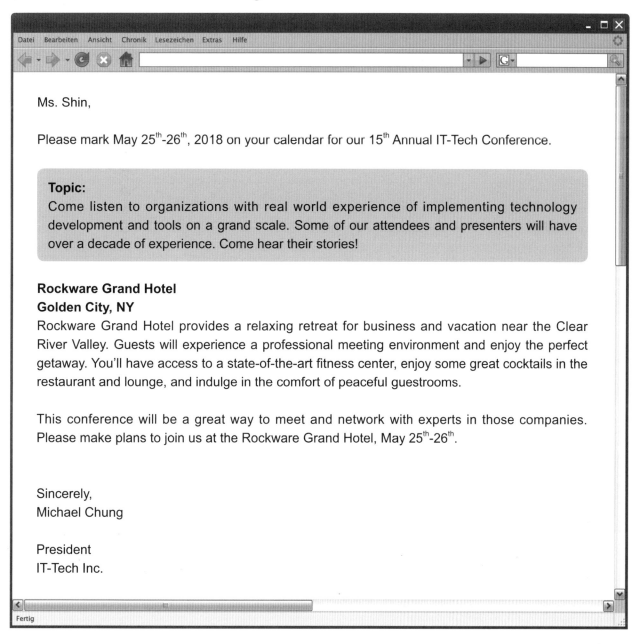

Ms. Shin,

Please mark May 25th-26th, 2018 on your calendar for our 15th Annual IT-Tech Conference.

> **Topic:**
> Come listen to organizations with real world experience of implementing technology development and tools on a grand scale. Some of our attendees and presenters will have over a decade of experience. Come hear their stories!

Rockware Grand Hotel
Golden City, NY
Rockware Grand Hotel provides a relaxing retreat for business and vacation near the Clear River Valley. Guests will experience a professional meeting environment and enjoy the perfect getaway. You'll have access to a state-of-the-art fitness center, enjoy some great cocktails in the restaurant and lounge, and indulge in the comfort of peaceful guestrooms.

This conference will be a great way to meet and network with experts in those companies. Please make plans to join us at the Rockware Grand Hotel, May 25th-26th.

Sincerely,
Michael Chung

President
IT-Tech Inc.

149. How long does the conference last?
(A) Two days
(B) Two weeks
(C) Twelve days
(D) One day

150. What is indicated about the conference speakers?
(A) They are well seasoned.
(B) They are new in the industry.
(C) They all work at Rockware Grand Hotel.
(D) They also teach in universities.

151. Which hotel facility is NOT mentioned in the article?
    (A) Guestrooms
    (B) Fitness center
    (C) Restaurants
    (D) ATM machines

Questions 152 - 153 refer to the following message chain.

Customer enquiry 3:05 p.m.	Hello! I'd like to learn more about the one-bedroom studio rental you have advertised on the website. My name is Jerry Lin. [1]
Service rep 3:06 p.m.	Yes. How can I help you, Jerry?
Customer enquiry 3:07 p.m.	So is the room still available?
Service rep 3:08 p.m.	I'm sorry, but that one-bedroom studio has been rented just this morning.
Customer enquiry 3:08 p.m.	Oh, that's too bad. [2]
Service rep 3:09 p.m.	We do have other rooms available. Would you like to check them out?
Customer enquiry 3:11 p.m.	Okay, we need to make an appointment or something? [3]
Service rep 3:12 p.m.	Yes, please. The Best Rental Agency is open Monday through Friday from 10 a.m. to 5 p.m. How about we make an appointment for this afternoon?
Customer enquiry 3:13 p.m.	It's okay. I think I'll go tomorrow at around 11 a.m. [4]
Service rep 3:15 p.m.	Sure. I'll be waiting for you, Jerry. By the way, I'm Emily Smith.

152. What is Jerry trying to do?
    (A) Apply for a new job
    (B) Purchase a new smartphone
    (C) Rent an apartment
    (D) File a complaint

153. In which of the positions marked [1], [2], [3], and [4] does the following sentence best belong?
    "What are your business hours?"
    (A) [1]
    (B) [2]
    (C) [3]
    (D) [4]

from a personal point of view

Questions 154 - 156 refer to the following article.

From the Admissions Office 入學審查委員會
January 23, 2018

Dear Students:

Researching and applying to business school can be a time-consuming process.
As you're making this decision, it's also important to think about how you're going to
finance your MBA. Here are a few tips to help you get a head start on the financial aid process:

Are you capable of ~

- **Check your credit report** – You don't want any surprises when you begin the loan application process, so it's important to know in advance where you stand with the credit rating agencies.
- **Research federal and private loan options** – There are a lot of different <u>loan programs</u>, so it's important to find the one that offers the best rates and is the best fit for you. If you have additional questions about financial aid options, please <u>visit our website</u>.
- **Research scholarships and industry-specific programs** – There are several <u>scholarship search engines</u> that will help you find organizations that may help you fund your MBA.

We hope this information is helpful. Next month, we will discuss in the newsletter the topic of admissions interviews.

Admissions Office
Linden School of Management
123-489-3327, Admissions Office   *interest rate*
123-489-2326, Visitor Center   利(息)率
123-489-7004, Fax
mba@linden.edu (Executive) Master of Business Administration. (EMBA)
                有工作經驗   高管碩士學院

154. Whom is this message intended for?
(A) Business students
(B) Accountants
(C) Fundraisers
(D) Website designers

155. How can interested students find out more about scholarship programs?
(A) Visit the Admissions Office in person
(B) Take advantage of scholarship search engines
(C) Ask professors to provide more information
(D) Check credit reports first

156. What is most likely the topic for next month's newsletter?
(A) MBA outlooks
(B) Future trends
(C) Successful interviews
(D) Correct investments

Questions 157 - 158 refer to the following letter.

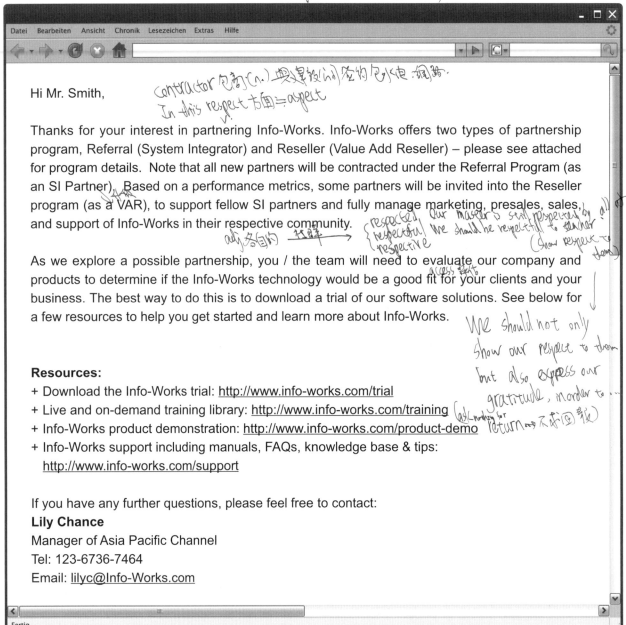

Hi Mr. Smith,

Thanks for your interest in partnering Info-Works. Info-Works offers two types of partnership program, Referral (System Integrator) and Reseller (Value Add Reseller) – please see attached for program details. Note that all new partners will be contracted under the Referral Program (as an SI Partner). Based on a performance metrics, some partners will be invited into the Reseller program (as a VAR), to support fellow SI partners and fully manage marketing, presales, sales, and support of Info-Works in their respective community.

As we explore a possible partnership, you / the team will need to evaluate our company and products to determine if the Info-Works technology would be a good fit for your clients and your business. The best way to do this is to download a trial of our software solutions. See below for a few resources to help you get started and learn more about Info-Works.

Resources:
+ Download the Info-Works trial: http://www.info-works.com/trial
+ Live and on-demand training library: http://www.info-works.com/training
+ Info-Works product demonstration: http://www.info-works.com/product-demo
+ Info-Works support including manuals, FAQs, knowledge base & tips:
   http://www.info-works.com/support

If you have any further questions, please feel free to contact:
Lily Chance
Manager of Asia Pacific Channel
Tel: 123-6736-7464
Email: lilyc@Info-Works.com

157. What can be inferred about Mr. Smith?
   (A) He wants to know where to download the software.
   (B) He will visit Ms. Chance in person next month.
   (C) He would like Info-Works to distribute his products.
   (D) He is interested in Info-Works' partnership program.

158. The word "evaluate" in paragraph 2, line 1, is closest in meaning to
   (A) simplify
   (B) assess
   (C) perform
   (D) participate

Questions 159 - 161 refer to the following letter.

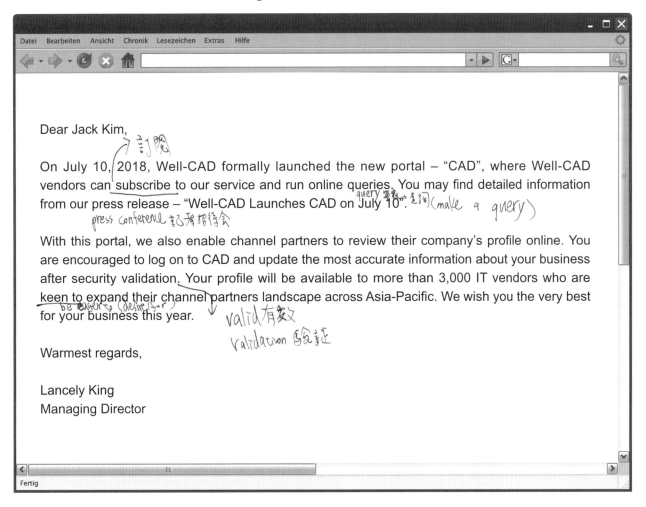

Dear Jack Kim,

On July 10, 2018, Well-CAD formally launched the new portal – "CAD", where Well-CAD vendors can subscribe to our service and run online queries. You may find detailed information from our press release – "Well-CAD Launches CAD on July 10".

With this portal, we also enable channel partners to review their company's profile online. You are encouraged to log on to CAD and update the most accurate information about your business after security validation. Your profile will be available to more than 3,000 IT vendors who are keen to expand their channel partners landscape across Asia-Pacific. We wish you the very best for your business this year.

Warmest regards,

Lancely King
Managing Director

159. What is the main topic of this message?
   (A) The announcement of a new portal for vendors
   (B) The invitation to a press conference
   (C) The news of a company acquisition
   (D) The release of a new software product

160. Who is most likely Jack Kim?
   (A) Lancely King's close friends
   (B) Lancely King's business partner
   (C) Lancely King's attorney
   (D) Lancely King's relative

161. What is the benefit for vendors to log on to CAD portal?
   (A) Other vendors can find them easily online.
   (B) They can post their product release online.
   (C) They can compare prices online.
   (D) Clients in the US can place orders online.

Questions 162 - 164 refer to the following letter.

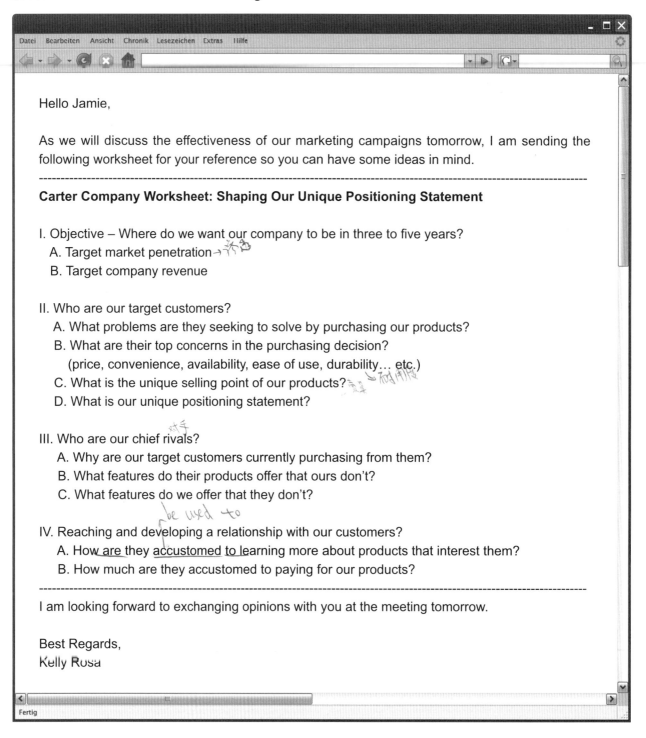

Hello Jamie,

As we will discuss the effectiveness of our marketing campaigns tomorrow, I am sending the following worksheet for your reference so you can have some ideas in mind.

Carter Company Worksheet: Shaping Our Unique Positioning Statement

I. Objective – Where do we want our company to be in three to five years?
　A. Target market penetration
　B. Target company revenue

II. Who are our target customers?
　A. What problems are they seeking to solve by purchasing our products?
　B. What are their top concerns in the purchasing decision?
　　(price, convenience, availability, ease of use, durability… etc.)
　C. What is the unique selling point of our products?
　D. What is our unique positioning statement?

III. Who are our chief rivals?
　A. Why are our target customers currently purchasing from them?
　B. What features do their products offer that ours don't?
　C. What features do we offer that they don't?

IV. Reaching and developing a relationship with our customers?
　A. How are they accustomed to learning more about products that interest them?
　B. How much are they accustomed to paying for our products?

I am looking forward to exchanging opinions with you at the meeting tomorrow.

Best Regards,
Kelly Rosa

162. According to the letter, what can be inferred about Jamie?
(A) She will have a meeting with Kelly tomorrow.
(B) She will fly to Japan for a conference next week.
(C) She doesn't know about their chief rival that much.
(D) She is in charge of arranging seminars.

163. What is most likely Kelly Rosa's job?
(A) Developing new product lines
(B) Planning new marketing strategies
(C) Dealing with customer complaints
(D) Directing company employees

164. What does Kelly Rosa want to know about customers?
(A) How customers would like to pay for products
(B) Where customers usually do their shopping
(C) The ways customers find products to fulfill their needs
(D) Why customers are not satisfied with their products

Questions 165 - 167 refer to the following advertisement.

Prepare for Business School

Getting into business school is not enough. You must succeed once you get there.

[1] Business Horizon teaches thousands of students how to excel in business school. We offer weeklong, intensive summer preparation courses in major cities in Taiwan. [2] For the past eight years, more than 90% of our surveyed students have said they would recommend Business Horizon to entering business students.

Attend Business Horizon now
* Receive over 30 hours of intensive instruction from the nation's top business professors [3]
* Master our unique test-taking method and apply it to real business school exams
* Understand academic strategies used by the most successful business students
* Enjoy exclusive discounts on books and study aids

[4] To register online, visit www.business-horizon.com.tw or call 1-800-3728-3847.

165. What is the purpose of this message?
   (A) To recruit business students
   (B) To enlist new soldiers
   (C) To promote a new product
   (D) To inform students of a course change

166. The word "intensive" in paragraph 2, line 2, is
   closest in meaning to
   (A) renewed
   (B) customized
   (C) concentrated
   (D) attentive

167. In which of the positions marked [1], [2], [3],
   and [4] does the following sentence best
   belong?
   **"For further information, feel free to contact
   Carol Kelly at ck@good-mail.com."**
   (A) [1]
   (B) [2]
   (C) [3]
   (D) [4]

Questions 168 - 170 refer to the following article.

Restaurant Review by Abel Milton

The Tasty Grill
182 2nd Ave., 3282-3849
All major credit cards
11 a.m. to 10 p.m., closed Monday
Reservations recommended

The two-month-old restaurant has attracted attention because of positive word-of-mouth on the Internet. The décor is charming and warm in an American country style. The menu is also very American and extensive.

The most delicious main course we tried was the country stew which consisted of potatoes, carrots, mushroom, and very tender beef. Because top quality beef was used, it was surprisingly good. Among other well-prepared main courses was the fried chicken. It was fresh and crisp. The vegetables that came with the main courses were fresh but a bit overcooked.

Because the main courses are large enough, there is no real need for an appetizer or soup. But for big eaters, I recommend the mixed salad. If you can still eat dessert after all these, try the apple pie. The apples were juicy and firm, and the pastry was light.

When I went at 7 p.m., it was so crowded that service was a bit slow. The reservation system didn't seem to work fine. Someone took our reservation for dinner, but the system didn't have it when we arrived. This kind of mistake can damage its reputation, although its food may be good.

168. What kind of food does the restaurant serve?
(A) Italian food
(B) Japanese food
(C) American food
(D) Chinese food

169. How old is the Tasty Grill?
(A) Two years old
(B) Two and half months old
(C) Three weeks old
(D) Two months old

170. What does the reviewer say about the main courses?
(A) They are overcooked.
(B) They are large meals.
(C) They are not as delicious as salad.
(D) They are not recommended.

Questions 171 - 175 refer to the following article.

Becoming a Springfield cab driver or hackie isn't all that easy. In order to get a license to drive a taxi in Springfield, candidates have to pass a detailed examination. They have to learn not only the streets, landmarks, and hotels, but also the best way to get to them. They are examined not only on the routes, but also on the best routes at different times of day. Springfield cabs don't have meters. Passengers are charged according to how many zones they are driven through. So candidates have to learn all the zones and the rates. People who want to pass the examinations spend much of their free time driving around Springfield, studying maps, and learning the street directory by heart.

171. What should candidates do to receive a taxi license in Springfield?
(A) Pass a comprehensive exam
(B) Buy a taxi
(C) Memorize all traffic rules
(D) Fill out an application form

172. What is indicated about becoming a taxi driver in Springfield?
(A) It's a dangerous job.
(B) It's not as simple as expected.
(C) It's rather easy.
(D) It takes more than two years to apply.

173. What is NOT mentioned as an element for taxi drivers to learn?
(A) Street names
(B) The best way to get to the destination
(C) Major landmarks
(D) Various payment methods

174. According to the article, how are passengers being charged?
(A) Based on cab meters
(B) Based on driver's experience
(C) Based on the number of zones
(D) Based on the size of the cab

175. What should candidates do in order to pass
the exam?
(A) Get familiar with roads in Springfield
(B) Call the city government to apply
(C) Participate in a seminar
(D) Discuss routes with passengers

Questions 176 - 180 refer to the following letters.

113 Elm Street
Taipei, Taiwan, 115

January 21, 2018

Customer Manager, Rosewater Motel
383 High Drive, Singapore

Dear Manager,

I am writing in reference to some laundry items which were lost and damaged during my last stay there. When my laundry was returned on December 16 of last year, which was the day I checked out, I found that two socks, one brown and one black, were missing. Also a shirt, which had been white, was a sickly blue. The housekeeper, to whom I complained, assured me that the missing socks would be mailed to me along with a check for $50 to cover the cost of the damaged shirt, which I had bought only a few days before.

More than a month has passed, and I still haven't received anything.

Thank you for your attention to this matter.

Sincerely yours,
Tim Lin

Rosewater Motel
383 High Drive, Singapore
123-2840-3828

February 10, 2018

Mr. Tim Lin
113 Elm Street
Taipei, Taiwan, 115

Dear Mr. Lin,

Thank you for your letter of January 21 in which you asked about missing and damaged laundry items while staying at our motel.

We regret that we are unable to trace the items to which you refer. The housekeeper to whom you spoke is no longer working with us. May we remind you that the form on which you listed your laundry states clearly that the motel is not responsible for loss or damage. The plastic bag in which you placed your clothes has the same warning printed in large letters on it.

We apologize for any inconvenience and hope that you will be staying with us again in the near future.

Sincerely yours,
Angie Glad

176. Why does Tim Lin write to Rosewater Motel?
    (A) To suggest a partnership formation
    (B) To file a complaint
    (C) To thank for their good service
    (D) To make a reservation

177. What was the original color of Tim's shirt?
    (A) White
    (B) Blue
    (C) Black
    (D) Brown

178. What did the housekeeper claim?
    (A) A thank-you note will be sent to Tim.
    (B) A new pair of socks will be sent to Tim.
    (C) A hotel voucher will be sent to Tim.
    (D) A $50 check will be sent to Tim.

179. Who is most likely Angie Glad?
    (A) Rosewater Motel customer care manager
    (B) Mr. Tim Lin's secretary
    (C) Rosewater Motel housekeeper
    (D) Mr. Tim Lin's housekeeper

180. What does Angie Glad claim?
   (A) The motel is not responsible for the loss.
   (B) The motel will send a new shirt to Mr. Lin soon.
   (C) The motel is happy to offer Mr. Lin a discount for his next stay.
   (D) The motel will keep looking for Mr. Lin's socks.

Questions 181 - 185 refer to the following emails.

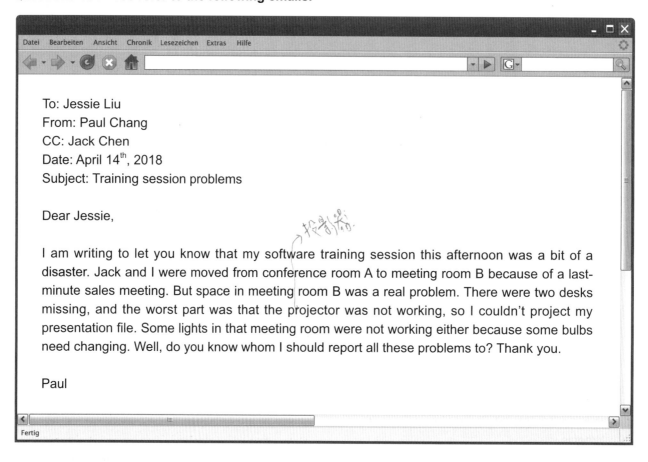

To: Jessie Liu
From: Paul Chang
CC: Jack Chen
Date: April 14th, 2018
Subject: Training session problems

Dear Jessie,

I am writing to let you know that my software training session this afternoon was a bit of a disaster. Jack and I were moved from conference room A to meeting room B because of a last-minute sales meeting. But space in meeting room B was a real problem. There were two desks missing, and the worst part was that the projector was not working, so I couldn't project my presentation file. Some lights in that meeting room were not working either because some bulbs need changing. Well, do you know whom I should report all these problems to? Thank you.

Paul

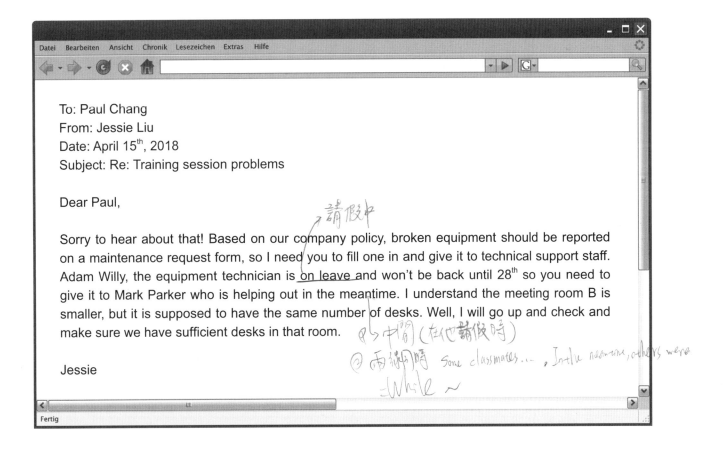

To: Paul Chang
From: Jessie Liu
Date: April 15th, 2018
Subject: Re: Training session problems

Dear Paul,

Sorry to hear about that! Based on our company policy, broken equipment should be reported on a maintenance request form, so I need you to fill one in and give it to technical support staff. Adam Willy, the equipment technician is on leave and won't be back until 28th so you need to give it to Mark Parker who is helping out in the meantime. I understand the meeting room B is smaller, but it is supposed to have the same number of desks. Well, I will go up and check and make sure we have sufficient desks in that room.

Jessie

181. What is true about Paul Chang?
(A) Paul was trying to arrange a meeting with Jack.
(B) His training session did not go well at all.
(C) He liked the environment in meeting room B.
(D) He liked the performance of the new projector.

182. What is wrong with lights in meeting room B?
(A) Some lights are missing.
(B) Some light bulbs need to be changed.
(C) Some lights are not energy efficient.
(D) Some lights are moved to meeting room A.

183. Whom should Paul give the maintenance request form to?
(A) Jessie Liu
(B) Jack Chen
(C) Adam Willy
(D) Mark Parker

184. What does Jessie offer to do?
(A) Check the number of desks in meeting room B
(B) Call Adam Willy to come back soon
(C) Reschedule Paul Chang's presentation
(D) Buy a new projector

185. In the second email, the word "maintenance" in paragraph 1, line 2, is closest in meaning to
(A) upkeep
(B) distribution
(C) development
(D) establishment

Questions 186 - 190 refer to the following press release and letters.

Digi-Tech Celebrates 20th Anniversary!

May 10th, 2018, Good Town, NM – Digi-Tech Inc. is proud to announce its twentieth year as the leading developer of accounting software. Digi-Tech Inc. has achieved two decades of innovation and steady growth. Digi-Tech's early success of @Easy software indicated a growing demand for user-friendly accounting tools. Most recently, the company has introduced @Efficient, which adds more powerful functions.

Digi-Tech's continual upgrading of existing products reflects the company's ongoing commitment to delivering innovative and powerful solution for accounting application. "Digi-Tech's success and longevity is due in part to the continuous improvement of our products," states VP of Sales Jack Jefferson.

To kick off its anniversary celebration, Digi-Tech will host a celebration party on Friday, June 18th. For details, visit Digi-Tech company website at www.digitech.com or call Eva Chen, PR Specialist at 800-333-9483.

May 15th, 2018

David Clark
1138 Goodway Road
Good Town, NM 83817

Dear Mr. Clark,

Digi-Tech is having a party on Friday, June 18th to celebrate our 20th anniversary of doing business. As you are our trusted customer, we would very much like for you to attend. It would be our great pleasure to have your participation.

The celebration party will be held at the Green Tree Inn, located on the south-east corner of 4th Street and 5th Avenue. Refreshments will be served at 6:00 p.m. and dinner will start at 8:00 p.m.

I hope you will be able to attend. Please relay your reply to me at your earliest convenience.

Thank you and we are looking forward to seeing you there.

Best regards,
Molly Perez
Digi-Tech Inc.

May 20th, 2018

Molly Perez
Digi-Tech Inc.
4732 Business Road
Good Town, NM 83817

Dear Ms. Perez,

I am delighted by your invitation to attend your company's party. Although I expect your party to be fun and a good opportunity to make business connections, I cannot attend it as I will be traveling to Singapore for a conference at the time.

Thank you for inviting me once again and I wish Digi-Tech Inc. the best in the future.

Sincerely,
David Clark

186. According to the press, which of the following statements about Digi-Tech is NOT true?
(A) It started its business twenty years ago.
(B) It has only a few employees.
(C) It's a software development company.
(D) It releases new products continuously.

187. Why does Molly Perez write to David Clark?
(A) To invite him to attend a webinar
(B) To place an order
(C) To invite him to attend a company celebration
(D) To inform him of a job opening

188. What does Molly Perez ask David Clark to do next?
(A) Confirm his attendance
(B) Submit an application form
(C) Return her call tomorrow
(D) Arrange a meeting at the Green Tree Inn

189. What does David Clark think of the party?
(A) The cost is too high.
(B) It's not fun at all.
(C) Party food is not that delicious.
(D) People can socialize with other business counterparts.

190. Why can't David Clark attend the event?
(A) Because he is too tired to go.
(B) Because he will be traveling then.
(C) Because his wife won't allow it.
(D) Because he doesn't know where the party will be held.

Questions 191 - 195 refer to the following memo, document, and email.

Office Memo

To: Grace Evans, Mark Wood, Tina Diaz, May Bailey
From: Will Nelson, VP of Sales and Marketing
Subject: Meeting for the comprehensive strategies of company's development

This is to inform you that our monthly review meeting will be conducted on Wednesday, June 13th, 2018. In addition to reviewing the assignments from our last meeting, we will also discuss more ways to generate sales leads in order to grow the company in this competitive market. Therefore, I request that you all attend the meeting without any fail. I would also like to request that you all present your plans and ideas on the company and team's growth. For any doubts or queries, contact my assistant within two working days.

Wuta Corp.
Meeting Minutes

Date: Wednesday, June 13th, 2018

Attendance
- Grace Evans, Marketing Specialist
- Mark Wood, Account Sales Representative
- Tina Diaz, Technical Support Engineer
- May Bailey, Customer Service Representative

Meeting Location
- Building: Eastern Hall B
- Meeting Room: A372

Meeting Start
- Meeting Schedule Start: Wednesday, June 13th, 3 p.m.
- Meeting Actual Start: Wednesday, June 13th, 3:15 p.m.
- Minutes Taker: Linda Carter

Agenda
- Review assignments from last meeting in May
- Review sales records of last week and identify prospective leads
- Plan Q3 marketing activities to generate sales leads
- Go through customer survey results

Meeting End
- Meeting Schedule End: 4:30 p.m.
- Meeting Actual End: 4:15 p.m.

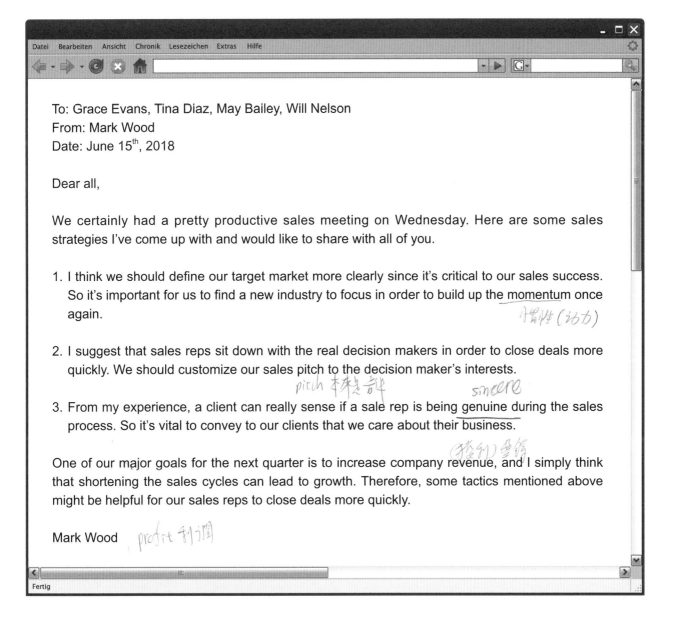

To: Grace Evans, Tina Diaz, May Bailey, Will Nelson
From: Mark Wood
Date: June 15th, 2018

Dear all,

We certainly had a pretty productive sales meeting on Wednesday. Here are some sales strategies I've come up with and would like to share with all of you.

1. I think we should define our target market more clearly since it's critical to our sales success. So it's important for us to find a new industry to focus in order to build up the momentum once again.

2. I suggest that sales reps sit down with the real decision makers in order to close deals more quickly. We should customize our sales pitch to the decision maker's interests.

3. From my experience, a client can really sense if a sale rep is being genuine during the sales process. So it's vital to convey to our clients that we care about their business.

One of our major goals for the next quarter is to increase company revenue, and I simply think that shortening the sales cycles can lead to growth. Therefore, some tactics mentioned above might be helpful for our sales reps to close deals more quickly.

Mark Wood

191. What's the purpose of the scheduled meeting?
    (A) To review customers' feedback
    (B) To brainstorm new product ideas
    (C) To discuss company's future development
    (D) To interview some applicants

192. What will NOT be discussed at the meeting?
    (A) Training workshops for customers
    (B) Opinions from each attendee
    (C) The assignments from last meeting
    (D) Ways to generate sales leads

193. What are the attendees required to do in the meeting?
    (A) Call and invite customers to join the meeting
    (B) Contribute good ideas
    (C) Bring lunch to share with others
    (D) Print out PPT files

194. What is most likely Grace Evans' job responsibility?
    (A) Answer technical phone calls
    (B) Plan marketing activities
    (C) Deal with angry customers
    (D) Hire new employees

195. What does Mark Wood mean when he says, "We should customize sales pitch"?
(A) In order to raise the points that decision makers really care about
(B) In order to attract more new customers from worldwide
(C) In order to come up with more marketing strategies
(D) In order to increase the meeting efficiency

Questions 196 - 200 refer to the following advertisement and letters.

Welcome to the Seaside Hotel

Seaside Hotel is just one block from the beach, and ten-minute driving from the charming downtown area. With shopping and dining and a great selection of outdoor activities only minutes away, you'll be in the center of it all.

With freshly baked cookies at check-in and our deluxe continental breakfast, all our guests will be taken care of at the Seaside Hotel. We have an indoor heated pool and an excellent group of hospitality experts dedicated to fulfilling all your lodging demands.

Each of our 50 spacious rooms and suites includes Wi-Fi, a refrigerator and a coffee maker. Complimentary movie rentals are also available. The Seaside Hotel is your hotel destination for a relaxing coastal vacation.

Amenities: Complimentary continental breakfast, Wireless Internet access, Warm cookies, Business center, Dry cleaning, Newspapers, Vehicle Parking.

To reserve online, please visit: http://www.seaside-hotel.com or call 800-383-5555.

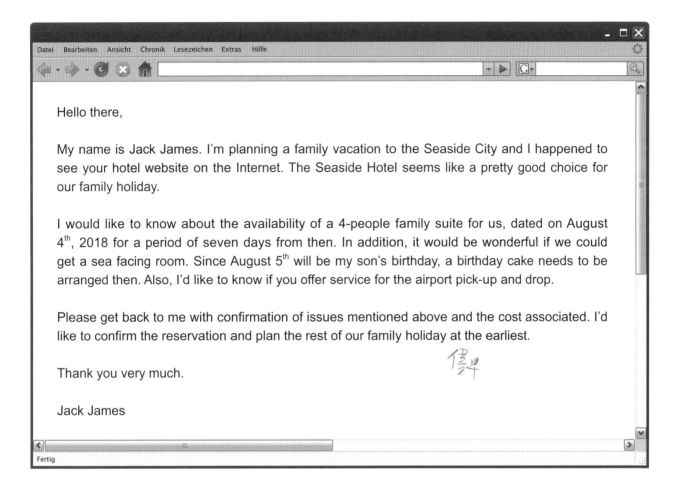

Hello there,

My name is Jack James. I'm planning a family vacation to the Seaside City and I happened to see your hotel website on the Internet. The Seaside Hotel seems like a pretty good choice for our family holiday.

I would like to know about the availability of a 4-people family suite for us, dated on August 4th, 2018 for a period of seven days from then. In addition, it would be wonderful if we could get a sea facing room. Since August 5th will be my son's birthday, a birthday cake needs to be arranged then. Also, I'd like to know if you offer service for the airport pick-up and drop.

Please get back to me with confirmation of issues mentioned above and the cost associated. I'd like to confirm the reservation and plan the rest of our family holiday at the earliest.

Thank you very much.

Jack James

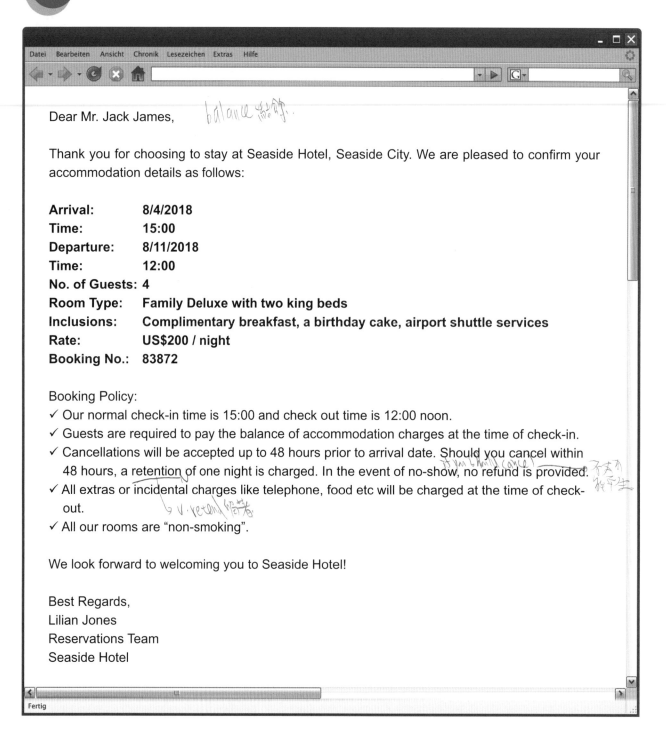

Dear Mr. Jack James,

Thank you for choosing to stay at Seaside Hotel, Seaside City. We are pleased to confirm your accommodation details as follows:

Arrival:	**8/4/2018**
Time:	**15:00**
Departure:	**8/11/2018**
Time:	**12:00**
No. of Guests:	**4**
Room Type:	**Family Deluxe with two king beds**
Inclusions:	**Complimentary breakfast, a birthday cake, airport shuttle services**
Rate:	**US$200 / night**
Booking No.:	**83872**

Booking Policy:
- ✓ Our normal check-in time is 15:00 and check out time is 12:00 noon.
- ✓ Guests are required to pay the balance of accommodation charges at the time of check-in.
- ✓ Cancellations will be accepted up to 48 hours prior to arrival date. Should you cancel within 48 hours, a retention of one night is charged. In the event of no-show, no refund is provided.
- ✓ All extras or incidental charges like telephone, food etc will be charged at the time of check-out.
- ✓ All our rooms are "non-smoking".

We look forward to welcoming you to Seaside Hotel!

Best Regards,
Lilian Jones
Reservations Team
Seaside Hotel

196. What is true about Seaside Hotel?
    (A) It's located on the high mountain.
    (B) It's a famous historical site.
    (C) It's near the beach.
    (D) It's a 2-star hotel.

197. What's the purpose of Jack James' letter?
    (A) To make a hotel reservation
    (B) To request product samples
    (C) To cancel his restaurant reservation
    (D) To arrange a birthday party

198. How does Jack James learn about the Seaside Hotel?
    (A) Through friend recommendations
    (B) On the web
    (C) In the newspaper
    (D) From one of his relatives

199. How much does Jack James need to pay for the hotel accommodation in total?
    (A) US$1,200
    (B) US$1,700
    (C) US$2,000
    (D) US$1,400

200. In the letter from Lilian Jones, the word "incidental" in paragraph 3, line 6, is closest in meaning to
    (A) related
    (B) inevitable
    (C) attractive
    (D) impossible

NEW TOEIC

Test 3

SAMPLE

TOEIC

★ Use only pencil
★ Darken the circles completely
★ Erase cleanly

MARKING DIRECTIONS

CORRECT MARK   INCORRECT MARKS

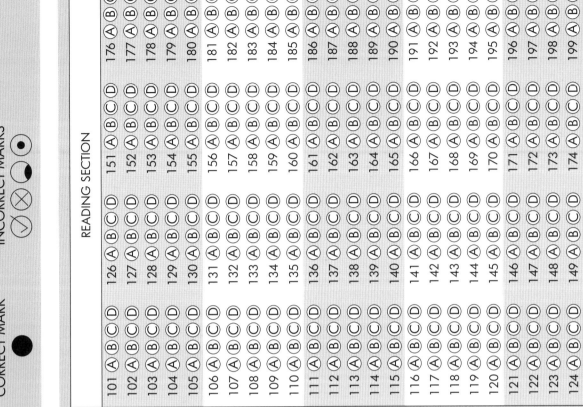

READING SECTION

101 Ⓐ Ⓑ Ⓒ Ⓓ	126 Ⓐ Ⓑ Ⓒ Ⓓ	151 Ⓐ Ⓑ Ⓒ Ⓓ	176 Ⓐ Ⓑ Ⓒ Ⓓ
102 Ⓐ Ⓑ Ⓒ Ⓓ	127 Ⓐ Ⓑ Ⓒ Ⓓ	152 Ⓐ Ⓑ Ⓒ Ⓓ	177 Ⓐ Ⓑ Ⓒ Ⓓ
103 Ⓐ Ⓑ Ⓒ Ⓓ	128 Ⓐ Ⓑ Ⓒ Ⓓ	153 Ⓐ Ⓑ Ⓒ Ⓓ	178 Ⓐ Ⓑ Ⓒ Ⓓ
104 Ⓐ Ⓑ Ⓒ Ⓓ	129 Ⓐ Ⓑ Ⓒ Ⓓ	154 Ⓐ Ⓑ Ⓒ Ⓓ	179 Ⓐ Ⓑ Ⓒ Ⓓ
105 Ⓐ Ⓑ Ⓒ Ⓓ	130 Ⓐ Ⓑ Ⓒ Ⓓ	155 Ⓐ Ⓑ Ⓒ Ⓓ	180 Ⓐ Ⓑ Ⓒ Ⓓ
106 Ⓐ Ⓑ Ⓒ Ⓓ	131 Ⓐ Ⓑ Ⓒ Ⓓ	156 Ⓐ Ⓑ Ⓒ Ⓓ	181 Ⓐ Ⓑ Ⓒ Ⓓ
107 Ⓐ Ⓑ Ⓒ Ⓓ	132 Ⓐ Ⓑ Ⓒ Ⓓ	157 Ⓐ Ⓑ Ⓒ Ⓓ	182 Ⓐ Ⓑ Ⓒ Ⓓ
108 Ⓐ Ⓑ Ⓒ Ⓓ	133 Ⓐ Ⓑ Ⓒ Ⓓ	158 Ⓐ Ⓑ Ⓒ Ⓓ	183 Ⓐ Ⓑ Ⓒ Ⓓ
109 Ⓐ Ⓑ Ⓒ Ⓓ	134 Ⓐ Ⓑ Ⓒ Ⓓ	159 Ⓐ Ⓑ Ⓒ Ⓓ	184 Ⓐ Ⓑ Ⓒ Ⓓ
110 Ⓐ Ⓑ Ⓒ Ⓓ	135 Ⓐ Ⓑ Ⓒ Ⓓ	160 Ⓐ Ⓑ Ⓒ Ⓓ	185 Ⓐ Ⓑ Ⓒ Ⓓ
111 Ⓐ Ⓑ Ⓒ Ⓓ	136 Ⓐ Ⓑ Ⓒ Ⓓ	161 Ⓐ Ⓑ Ⓒ Ⓓ	186 Ⓐ Ⓑ Ⓒ Ⓓ
112 Ⓐ Ⓑ Ⓒ Ⓓ	137 Ⓐ Ⓑ Ⓒ Ⓓ	162 Ⓐ Ⓑ Ⓒ Ⓓ	187 Ⓐ Ⓑ Ⓒ Ⓓ
113 Ⓐ Ⓑ Ⓒ Ⓓ	138 Ⓐ Ⓑ Ⓒ Ⓓ	163 Ⓐ Ⓑ Ⓒ Ⓓ	188 Ⓐ Ⓑ Ⓒ Ⓓ
114 Ⓐ Ⓑ Ⓒ Ⓓ	139 Ⓐ Ⓑ Ⓒ Ⓓ	164 Ⓐ Ⓑ Ⓒ Ⓓ	189 Ⓐ Ⓑ Ⓒ Ⓓ
115 Ⓐ Ⓑ Ⓒ Ⓓ	140 Ⓐ Ⓑ Ⓒ Ⓓ	165 Ⓐ Ⓑ Ⓒ Ⓓ	190 Ⓐ Ⓑ Ⓒ Ⓓ
116 Ⓐ Ⓑ Ⓒ Ⓓ	141 Ⓐ Ⓑ Ⓒ Ⓓ	166 Ⓐ Ⓑ Ⓒ Ⓓ	191 Ⓐ Ⓑ Ⓒ Ⓓ
117 Ⓐ Ⓑ Ⓒ Ⓓ	142 Ⓐ Ⓑ Ⓒ Ⓓ	167 Ⓐ Ⓑ Ⓒ Ⓓ	192 Ⓐ Ⓑ Ⓒ Ⓓ
118 Ⓐ Ⓑ Ⓒ Ⓓ	143 Ⓐ Ⓑ Ⓒ Ⓓ	168 Ⓐ Ⓑ Ⓒ Ⓓ	193 Ⓐ Ⓑ Ⓒ Ⓓ
119 Ⓐ Ⓑ Ⓒ Ⓓ	144 Ⓐ Ⓑ Ⓒ Ⓓ	169 Ⓐ Ⓑ Ⓒ Ⓓ	194 Ⓐ Ⓑ Ⓒ Ⓓ
120 Ⓐ Ⓑ Ⓒ Ⓓ	145 Ⓐ Ⓑ Ⓒ Ⓓ	170 Ⓐ Ⓑ Ⓒ Ⓓ	195 Ⓐ Ⓑ Ⓒ Ⓓ
121 Ⓐ Ⓑ Ⓒ Ⓓ	146 Ⓐ Ⓑ Ⓒ Ⓓ	171 Ⓐ Ⓑ Ⓒ Ⓓ	196 Ⓐ Ⓑ Ⓒ Ⓓ
122 Ⓐ Ⓑ Ⓒ Ⓓ	147 Ⓐ Ⓑ Ⓒ Ⓓ	172 Ⓐ Ⓑ Ⓒ Ⓓ	197 Ⓐ Ⓑ Ⓒ Ⓓ
123 Ⓐ Ⓑ Ⓒ Ⓓ	148 Ⓐ Ⓑ Ⓒ Ⓓ	173 Ⓐ Ⓑ Ⓒ Ⓓ	198 Ⓐ Ⓑ Ⓒ Ⓓ
124 Ⓐ Ⓑ Ⓒ Ⓓ	149 Ⓐ Ⓑ Ⓒ Ⓓ	174 Ⓐ Ⓑ Ⓒ Ⓓ	199 Ⓐ Ⓑ Ⓒ Ⓓ
125 Ⓐ Ⓑ Ⓒ Ⓓ	150 Ⓐ Ⓑ Ⓒ Ⓓ	175 Ⓐ Ⓑ Ⓒ Ⓓ	200 Ⓐ Ⓑ Ⓒ Ⓓ

LISTENING SECTION

1 Ⓐ Ⓑ Ⓒ Ⓓ	26 Ⓐ Ⓑ Ⓒ Ⓓ	51 Ⓐ Ⓑ Ⓒ Ⓓ	76 Ⓐ Ⓑ Ⓒ Ⓓ
2 Ⓐ Ⓑ Ⓒ Ⓓ	27 Ⓐ Ⓑ Ⓒ Ⓓ	52 Ⓐ Ⓑ Ⓒ Ⓓ	77 Ⓐ Ⓑ Ⓒ Ⓓ
3 Ⓐ Ⓑ Ⓒ Ⓓ	28 Ⓐ Ⓑ Ⓒ Ⓓ	53 Ⓐ Ⓑ Ⓒ Ⓓ	78 Ⓐ Ⓑ Ⓒ Ⓓ
4 Ⓐ Ⓑ Ⓒ Ⓓ	29 Ⓐ Ⓑ Ⓒ Ⓓ	54 Ⓐ Ⓑ Ⓒ Ⓓ	79 Ⓐ Ⓑ Ⓒ Ⓓ
5 Ⓐ Ⓑ Ⓒ Ⓓ	30 Ⓐ Ⓑ Ⓒ Ⓓ	55 Ⓐ Ⓑ Ⓒ Ⓓ	80 Ⓐ Ⓑ Ⓒ Ⓓ
6 Ⓐ Ⓑ Ⓒ Ⓓ	31 Ⓐ Ⓑ Ⓒ Ⓓ	56 Ⓐ Ⓑ Ⓒ Ⓓ	81 Ⓐ Ⓑ Ⓒ Ⓓ
7 Ⓐ Ⓑ Ⓒ Ⓓ	32 Ⓐ Ⓑ Ⓒ Ⓓ	57 Ⓐ Ⓑ Ⓒ Ⓓ	82 Ⓐ Ⓑ Ⓒ Ⓓ
8 Ⓐ Ⓑ Ⓒ Ⓓ	33 Ⓐ Ⓑ Ⓒ Ⓓ	58 Ⓐ Ⓑ Ⓒ Ⓓ	83 Ⓐ Ⓑ Ⓒ Ⓓ
9 Ⓐ Ⓑ Ⓒ Ⓓ	34 Ⓐ Ⓑ Ⓒ Ⓓ	59 Ⓐ Ⓑ Ⓒ Ⓓ	84 Ⓐ Ⓑ Ⓒ Ⓓ
10 Ⓐ Ⓑ Ⓒ Ⓓ	35 Ⓐ Ⓑ Ⓒ Ⓓ	60 Ⓐ Ⓑ Ⓒ Ⓓ	85 Ⓐ Ⓑ Ⓒ Ⓓ
11 Ⓐ Ⓑ Ⓒ Ⓓ	36 Ⓐ Ⓑ Ⓒ Ⓓ	61 Ⓐ Ⓑ Ⓒ Ⓓ	86 Ⓐ Ⓑ Ⓒ Ⓓ
12 Ⓐ Ⓑ Ⓒ Ⓓ	37 Ⓐ Ⓑ Ⓒ Ⓓ	62 Ⓐ Ⓑ Ⓒ Ⓓ	87 Ⓐ Ⓑ Ⓒ Ⓓ
13 Ⓐ Ⓑ Ⓒ Ⓓ	38 Ⓐ Ⓑ Ⓒ Ⓓ	63 Ⓐ Ⓑ Ⓒ Ⓓ	88 Ⓐ Ⓑ Ⓒ Ⓓ
14 Ⓐ Ⓑ Ⓒ Ⓓ	39 Ⓐ Ⓑ Ⓒ Ⓓ	64 Ⓐ Ⓑ Ⓒ Ⓓ	89 Ⓐ Ⓑ Ⓒ Ⓓ
15 Ⓐ Ⓑ Ⓒ Ⓓ	40 Ⓐ Ⓑ Ⓒ Ⓓ	65 Ⓐ Ⓑ Ⓒ Ⓓ	90 Ⓐ Ⓑ Ⓒ Ⓓ
16 Ⓐ Ⓑ Ⓒ Ⓓ	41 Ⓐ Ⓑ Ⓒ Ⓓ	66 Ⓐ Ⓑ Ⓒ Ⓓ	91 Ⓐ Ⓑ Ⓒ Ⓓ
17 Ⓐ Ⓑ Ⓒ Ⓓ	42 Ⓐ Ⓑ Ⓒ Ⓓ	67 Ⓐ Ⓑ Ⓒ Ⓓ	92 Ⓐ Ⓑ Ⓒ Ⓓ
18 Ⓐ Ⓑ Ⓒ Ⓓ	43 Ⓐ Ⓑ Ⓒ Ⓓ	68 Ⓐ Ⓑ Ⓒ Ⓓ	93 Ⓐ Ⓑ Ⓒ Ⓓ
19 Ⓐ Ⓑ Ⓒ Ⓓ	44 Ⓐ Ⓑ Ⓒ Ⓓ	69 Ⓐ Ⓑ Ⓒ Ⓓ	94 Ⓐ Ⓑ Ⓒ Ⓓ
20 Ⓐ Ⓑ Ⓒ Ⓓ	45 Ⓐ Ⓑ Ⓒ Ⓓ	70 Ⓐ Ⓑ Ⓒ Ⓓ	95 Ⓐ Ⓑ Ⓒ Ⓓ
21 Ⓐ Ⓑ Ⓒ Ⓓ	46 Ⓐ Ⓑ Ⓒ Ⓓ	71 Ⓐ Ⓑ Ⓒ Ⓓ	96 Ⓐ Ⓑ Ⓒ Ⓓ
22 Ⓐ Ⓑ Ⓒ Ⓓ	47 Ⓐ Ⓑ Ⓒ Ⓓ	72 Ⓐ Ⓑ Ⓒ Ⓓ	97 Ⓐ Ⓑ Ⓒ Ⓓ
23 Ⓐ Ⓑ Ⓒ Ⓓ	48 Ⓐ Ⓑ Ⓒ Ⓓ	73 Ⓐ Ⓑ Ⓒ Ⓓ	98 Ⓐ Ⓑ Ⓒ Ⓓ
24 Ⓐ Ⓑ Ⓒ Ⓓ	49 Ⓐ Ⓑ Ⓒ Ⓓ	74 Ⓐ Ⓑ Ⓒ Ⓓ	99 Ⓐ Ⓑ Ⓒ Ⓓ
25 Ⓐ Ⓑ Ⓒ Ⓓ	50 Ⓐ Ⓑ Ⓒ Ⓓ	75 Ⓐ Ⓑ Ⓒ Ⓓ	100 Ⓐ Ⓑ Ⓒ Ⓓ

TOEIC 分數試算參考表

聽力部分		閱讀部分	
答對題數	換算分數範圍	答對題數	換算分數範圍
96~100	475~495	96~100	455~495
91~95	440~480	91~95	415~460
86~90	415~460	86~90	390~435
81~85	380~430	81~85	360~405
76~80	350~405	76~80	330~380
71~75	320~370	71~75	300~350
66~70	290~340	66~70	270~320
61~65	260~310	61~65	235~280
56~60	240~280	56~60	205~250
51~55	210~260	51~55	175~220
46~50	190~230	46~50	150~190
41~45	165~210	41~45	125~165
36~40	145~185	36~40	105~145
31~35	120~165	31~35	85~125
26~30	100~140	26~30	60~100
21~25	75~120	21~25	45~80
16~20	50~100	16~20	30~65
11~15	30~70	11~15	20~55
6~10	10~50	6~10	15~40
1~5	5~30	1~5	5~20
0	5	0	5

Test 3 分數試算

	答對題數	換算分數範圍
Listening		
Reading		
Total Score		

In the Listening test, you are asked to demonstrate how well you understand spoken English. There are four parts to the test and directions are given for each part before it starts. The entire Listening test will last approximately 45 minutes. You must mark your answers on the separate answer sheet. Do not write your answers in your test book.

Part I. ▶ Photographs

曲目 9

Directions: For each question in this part, you will hear four statements about a picture in your test book. You must select the statement (A), (B), (C), or (D) that best describes the picture, and mark your answer on your answer sheet. The statements will not be printed in your test book and will be spoken only once. Look at the example picture below.

Example

You will hear:
Now listen to the four statements.
(A) The man is checking in.
(B) The man is applying for a job.
(C) The woman is not on duty.
(D) There are some pictures hanging on the wall.

Statement (A), "The man is checking in." is the best description of the picture, so you should mark answer (A) on your answer sheet. Now, Part One will begin.

1.

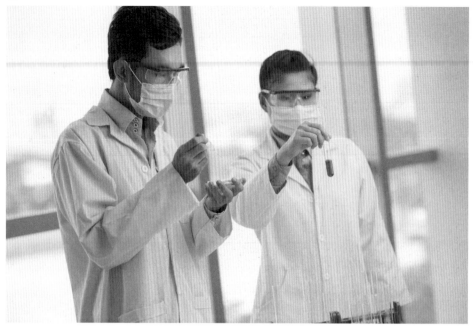

2.

3.

4.

5.

6.

Part II. ▶ Question-Response

曲目 10

Directions: You will hear a question or statement and three responses. Select the best response to the question or statement, and mark the letter (A), (B), or (C) on your answer sheet. The responses will not be printed in your test book and will be spoken only once.

Example

You will hear: How are you doing?
You will also hear:
(A) I'm doing okay. How are you?
(B) Oops, my bad.
(C) My company is making profits.

The best response to the question "How are you doing?" is choice (A) "I'm doing okay. How are you?" So (A) is the correct answer. You should mark answer (A) on your answer sheet. Now, Part Two will begin.

7. Mark your answer on your answer sheet.

8. Mark your answer on your answer sheet.

9. Mark your answer on your answer sheet.

10. Mark your answer on your answer sheet.

11. Mark your answer on your answer sheet.

12. Mark your answer on your answer sheet.

13. Mark your answer on your answer sheet.

14. Mark your answer on your answer sheet.

15. Mark your answer on your answer sheet.

16. Mark your answer on your answer sheet.

17. Mark your answer on your answer sheet.

18. Mark your answer on your answer sheet.

19. Mark your answer on your answer sheet.

20. Mark your answer on your answer sheet.

21. Mark your answer on your answer sheet.

22. Mark your answer on your answer sheet.

23. Mark your answer on your answer sheet.

24. Mark your answer on your answer sheet.

25. Mark your answer on your answer sheet.

26. Mark your answer on your answer sheet.

27. Mark your answer on your answer sheet.

28. Mark your answer on your answer sheet.

29. Mark your answer on your answer sheet.

30. Mark your answer on your answer sheet.

31. Mark your answer on your answer sheet.

Part III. ► Conversations

曲目 11

Directions: You will hear some conversations. For each conversation, you will be asked to answer three questions about what the speakers say. Select the best response to each question and mark the letter (A), (B), (C), or (D) on your answer sheet. The conversations will not be printed in your test book and will be spoken only once.

32. Who is most likely the woman?
(A) Mr. Jackson's assistant
(B) Mr. Chance's client
(C) Mr. Jackson's boss
(D) Mr. Chance's secretary

33. What would the man probably like to do?
(A) Visit his relatives
(B) Visit his customer
(C) Visit his doctor
(D) Visit his high school classmates

34. When will the man meet with Mr. Chance?
(A) Tomorrow morning at 10
(B) This afternoon at 2:30
(C) Tomorrow afternoon at 4
(D) Tomorrow afternoon at 2:30

35. Where does the conversation most likely take place?
(A) In a metro station
(B) On a beach
(C) In a conference room
(D) In a bank

36. Who is most likely the woman?
(A) An interviewer
(B) A customer service representative
(C) A city hall employee
(D) A broadcast announcer

37. What is the man's major concern?
(A) How much he needs to pay
(B) How fast he can get to the destination
(C) How far he needs to walk
(D) How often the metro train leaves

38. What is most likely the relationship between the two speakers?
(A) Husband and wife
(B) Professor and student
(C) Administrator and secretary
(D) Sales manager and client

39. What's the purpose of Ms. Smith's call?
(A) To propose a meeting
(B) To invite the man to attend a conference in Canada
(C) To check the CAI project
(D) To cancel an order

40. Why does North Systems want to cancel the order?
(A) Because they lost the CAI case
(B) Because their customers don't want it anymore
(C) Because they are short of money
(D) Because their customers are happy with the quality

41. Why does the man want to arrange this meeting?
(A) To interview some candidates
(B) To discuss some computer network problems
(C) To celebrate Tom's promotion
(D) To review the woman's performance

42. Who is Tom?
    (A) The sales manager
    (B) The network architect
    (C) The team leader
    (D) The VP of engineering

43. What will the woman probably do next?
    (A) Email Tom an agreement
    (B) Fax Phil the meeting agenda
    (C) Call and invite Tom to attend a meeting
    (D) Reschedule the meeting to next Friday

44. Where does the conversation probably take place?
    (A) A meeting point on the Internet
    (B) In Singapore
    (C) At an airport
    (D) In the woman's kitchen

45. What's both men's problem?
    (A) They didn't receive the meeting minutes.
    (B) They forgot to send out the meeting minutes.
    (C) Their email systems are not working properly.
    (D) They didn't send the contract to the woman.

46. How did the woman send out the minutes?
    (A) Via fax
    (B) Via email
    (C) Via courier
    (D) Via mail

47. Where does the conversation probably take place?
    (A) In a restaurant
    (B) In a supermarket
    (C) On a street
    (D) In a kitchen

48. Who is most likely the woman?
    (A) A cook
    (B) A student
    (C) A waitress
    (D) An actress

49. How does the man feel about the 10-minute wait?
    (A) He thinks it is annoying.
    (B) He thinks it is a good idea.
    (C) He will be cooking tonight.
    (D) It doesn't bother him that much.

50. Where is the man probably working?
    (A) In an Internet café
    (B) In a computer store
    (C) In a travel agency
    (D) In a hotel

51. Why does the woman call?
    (A) To make a room reservation
    (B) To cancel a meeting
    (C) To retrieve her ID number
    (D) To ask about the availability of a conference venue

52. When will the woman probably be checking out?
    (A) May 15th
    (B) May 30th
    (C) May 22nd
    (D) June 2nd

53. What are the two speakers talking about?
    (A) Customer survey results
    (B) Meeting arrangement
    (C) Lunch meeting
    (D) Travel plan

54. Why does the woman want to meet earlier?
    (A) Since she will be traveling next week
    (B) Since the man will visit clients next week
    (C) Since she will be busy next week
    (D) Since the man will have a meeting next week

55. When will the speakers meet?
    (A) This Friday afternoon
    (B) This Thursday morning
    (C) Next Wednesday afternoon
    (D) This Friday Morning

56. What's the purpose of the man's call?
    (A) To ask about an outstanding invoice
    (B) To request some product information
    (C) To invite the woman to attend a seminar
    (D) To arrange some shipments

57. Why does the woman's company delay the payment?
    (A) Because the accountant is on vacation
    (B) Because they don't have cash available
    (C) Because the bank won't lend them any more money
    (D) Because the woman has maxed out her credit cards

58. When will the woman's company expect to pay?
    (A) By the end of this month
    (B) By the end of the day
    (C) By the end of the week
    (D) Within three days

59. What are the two speakers doing?
    (A) Arranging a conference in Madison
    (B) Driving to New York
    (C) Purchasing plane tickets
    (D) Planning their weekend

60. How far is it from New York to Madison?
    (A) It takes 30 minutes by train.
    (B) It takes 10 minutes by car.
    (C) It takes 20 minutes on foot.
    (D) It takes 30 minutes by car.

61. What will the woman probably do next?
    (A) Plan the weekend with other friends
    (B) Drive to New York with the man
    (C) Go online to buy train tickets
    (D) Go to the East Station to take a train

62. Where does the conversation most likely take place?
    (A) By a beach
    (B) On a street
    (C) At an airport
    (D) In an office

63. What is the woman doing?
    (A) Attending a seminar
    (B) Taking some photos
    (C) Driving to a gas station
    (D) Asking for directions

64. Please look at the map. Which hotel does the woman probably live in?

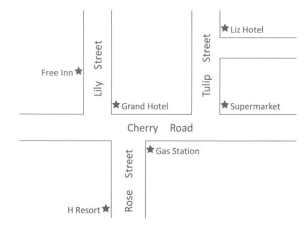

    (A) Liz Hotel
    (B) H Resort
    (C) Grand Hotel
    (D) Free Inn

65. What is the man's problem?
    (A) He missed the flight.
    (B) He arrived too early.
    (C) He lost his passport.
    (D) He doesn't know which gate to go.

66. What does the woman suggest the man do?
(A) Go to Gate 8 immediately
(B) Purchase another ticket
(C) Go to Chicago by train instead
(D) Take another flight next day

67. Please look at the table. Which flight will the man most likely take?

Flight Number	Date	Time	To	Status
A483	10/4	3 p.m.	Singapore	Delayed
H889	10/4	4:15 p.m.	Chicago	Departed
GR937	10/5	10 a.m.	Chicago	---
SI012	10/5	11:30 a.m.	New York	---

(A) SI012
(B) GR937
(C) A483
(D) H889

68. What is the woman going to do?
(A) Apply for a job
(B) Rent a car
(C) Reserve a room
(D) Arrange a meeting

69. What does the man suggest the woman do?
(A) Select a compact model
(B) Pay by credit card
(C) Search online first
(D) Renew her driver's license

70. Please look at the table. Which car would the woman most likely rent?

Car Number	Availability	Inclusion	Model
1	O	Automatic transmission, A/C, insurance	Lux
2	O	Automatic transmission, A/C	GM Compact
3	X	Automatic transmission	GM Standard
4	O	A/C	GM Compact

(A) 1
(B) 2
(C) 3
(D) 4

Part IV. ► Talks

曲目 12

Directions: You will hear some talks given by a single speaker. For each talk, you will be asked to answer three questions about what the speaker says. Select the best response to each question and mark the letter (A), (B), (C), or (D) on your answer sheet. The talks will not be printed in your test book and will be spoken only once.

71. According to the speaker, what will happen when a child is continually criticized?
(A) Fear, doubt, and worry will arise.
(B) Children will feel happy and optimistic.
(C) Their school performance will improve.
(D) They will never feel upset.

72. What is mentioned about parents in Taiwan?
(A) They tend to spoil their children.
(B) They praise their children a lot.
(C) They seldom express love to their children.
(D) They gratify their children's demands.

73. What will the speaker probably talk about next?
(A) How to gratify parents
(B) How and when to praise children
(C) How to build parents' confidence
(D) When to express love

74. What is the speaker's job?
(A) A professional speaker
(B) A technology consultant
(C) An R&D manager
(D) A product manager

75. Where does the speaker most likely live?
(A) In the US
(B) In Singapore
(C) In the UK
(D) In China

76. What is the speaker's main job responsibility?
(A) Study more software knowledge
(B) Manage an IT company
(C) Invent new cell phones
(D) Develop state-of-the-art products

77. Who is most likely the speaker?
(A) The chairperson
(B) A participant
(C) The general manager
(D) A consultant

78. What is the problem with the product launch?
(A) The general manager disagrees about the budget.
(B) Members disagree about the launch timeline.
(C) The new product launch will be delayed.
(D) The chairperson can't make a final decision.

79. When will the decision be finalized?
(A) Within this quarter
(B) Within this month
(C) Within this week
(D) Within two days

80. What was sent to the speaker yesterday by Jack?
(A) Hotel reservation confirmation
(B) Plane tickets
(C) Project contract
(D) Hotel list

81. When will the speaker probably check in?
(A) On May 21st
(B) On May 30th
(C) On May 25th
(D) On May 15th

82. How will Jack probably contact the speaker?
(A) Directly visit the speaker
(B) Via email
(C) By returning the call
(D) Via fax

83. Who are the guests on the program?
(A) Three female professors
(B) Three female entrepreneurs
(C) Three male directors
(D) Three male engineers

84. What is special about the three guests?
(A) They are all outstanding translators.
(B) They all won an award.
(C) They all know how to avoid risks.
(D) They all started their own businesses.

85. Who will probably speak next?
(A) Tom Brook
(B) Lisa Sweeney
(C) Avon Dignen
(D) Lorrie Flinders

86. What was the weather like yesterday?
(A) Sunny
(B) Rainy
(C) Snowy
(D) Windy

87. What will the weather be like tomorrow?
(A) Colder
(B) Warmer
(C) More humid
(D) Hotter

88. What is the audience asked to do?
(A) Get up earlier tomorrow morning
(B) Take an umbrella
(C) Keep listening to the program
(D) Wear a heavy coat

89. What is the workshop all about?
(A) How to live more happily
(B) How to hold productive meetings
(C) How to deliver a good speech
(D) How to deal with conflicts

90. What's one of the chairperson's duties?
(A) Disagree with all participants
(B) Make a final decision all by himself
(C) Be a good timekeeper
(D) Start the meeting late

91. What will the workshop participants do next?
(A) Have lunch together
(B) Have a long sales meeting
(C) Select a chairperson
(D) Contribute their ideas

92. What is the problem?
(A) Boarding will be delayed.
(B) Weather condition is bad.
(C) Passengers are too tired.
(D) Display screens are not working.

93. Where should passengers be waiting?
(A) Near the check-in counter
(B) Inside the aircraft
(C) Near Gate 73
(D) Outside the airport

94. What should passengers do if they have questions?
(A) Call their relatives
(B) Contact the staff
(C) Email the captain
(D) Call the airline company

95. What time is the man leaving the phone message?
(A) 2 p.m.
(B) 8:10 p.m.
(C) 3 a.m.
(D) 8:10 a.m.

96. Why does the speaker call Ms. Benchmark?
(A) He wants to cancel the meeting.
(B) He wants to schedule a con-call.
(C) He wants to reschedule the meeting.
(D) He wants to schedule a visit.

97. Please look at the table. When will they most likely meet?

Time	Wednesday	Thursday	Friday
9 a.m.	Sales Meeting	TDI Discussion	Client – Ms. Dan
11 a.m.	Mr. Jackson	Sales Strategies	PM Reports
1 p.m.	Budget Planning	n/a	Lunch Meeting
3 p.m.	Ticket Confirmation	n/a	n/a
5 p.m.	Con-call	Return Emails	n/a

(A) Friday afternoon at 3:30
(B) Thursday afternoon at 5
(C) Friday morning at 10
(D) Wednesday afternoon at 2

98. When does the talk most likely take place?
(A) During a resume-writing workshop
(B) During a presentation training course
(C) During a job interview
(D) During a technology conference

99. Please look at the CV. What position is the speaker applying for?

Lily Chang
Lily.chang@mail.com
Objective: Applying for the Product Manager position
Education: 1st major – Financial Management
2nd major – Technology Management
Training: Communication / Presentation Skills
Language: Fluent in English, Chinese and Japanese

(A) Product manager
(B) Sales representative
(C) TOEIC instructor
(D) Communication trainer

100. What will the speaker probably do next?
(A) Study technology management
(B) Answer some interview questions
(C) Ask the interviewer some questions
(D) Negotiate with Mr. Louis

In the Reading test, you are asked to demonstrate how well you understand written English. There are three parts to the test and directions are given for each part before it starts. The entire Reading test will last 75 minutes. You are encouraged to answer as many questions as possible within the time allowed. You must mark your answers on the separate answer sheet. Do not write your answers in your test book.

Part V. ▶ Incomplete Sentences

Directions: In this part, you will read several single sentences. For each sentence, a word or phrase is missing, and four answer choices are given. Select the best answer to complete the sentence, and mark the letter (A), (B), (C), or (D) on your answer sheet.

101. As people live hectic lives in this modern world, our minds are kept busy _____ what is going on around us.
(A) interpretation
(B) interpreting
(C) interpreter
(D) interpret

102. _____ you are nervous, you should sit somewhere comfortable where you won't be disturbed.
(A) When
(B) Although
(C) But
(D) However

103. One of our team members, Marian, _____ a collection of framed drawings in her office.
(A) have
(B) has
(C) having
(D) hasn't

104. We all know that the balance _____ work and other aspects of our life can have a huge impact on our health.
(A) with
(B) together
(C) between
(D) among

105. TakeNote's user-friendly screens allow _____ to analyze project risks and respond to potential problems.
(A) customs
(B) customers
(C) costumes
(D) copiers

106. There are speaking coaches who can teach leaders how to pitch their voice _____ they are able to control the room.
(A) ever since
(B) in spite of
(C) so that
(D) in order to

107. Studies have shown that constant interruptions are the most _____ element of a manager's day.
(A) annoy
(D) annoying
(C) annoyed
(D) annoyance

108. When you deal with a _____ customer, treat that customer as if he was a tired, hungry child who is becoming angry.
(A) difficult
(B) challenging
(C) hard
(D) troubled

109. Working from home one day a week is good for employees, but _____ their home can offer the necessary privacy.
(A) only
(B) only if
(C) even
(D) as well as

110. Our goal is to allow our customers to _____ shareholder value and improve end-user satisfaction.
(A) increase
(B) decrease
(C) fluctuate
(D) decline

111. Because of early childhood criticism, many people grow up _____ fears of rejection.
(A) of
(B) for
(C) in
(D) with

112. No one who _____ part of a team can work in isolation.
(A) is
(B) are
(C) were
(D) was

113. I am afraid we are running out of time, _____ we will have to stop our discussion.
(A) or
(B) and
(C) so
(D) but

114. Zenia and Alife had a discussion _____ the possibility of two companies working together.
(A) for
(B) about
(C) of
(D) with

115. If you offer more flexible payment _____, we will agree to place an order next week.
(A) conditions
(B) occasions
(C) guarantees
(D) procedures

116. For over ten years, CoreValue has _____ continuous year-over-year growth.
(A) experiences
(B) experienced
(C) experiencing
(D) experience

117. I am appointed to chair a meeting about the year-end party, but I am incredibly nervous as I've never _____ one before.
(A) chair
(B) chaired
(C) chairing
(D) chairman

118. _____ faced with a failed conversation, most people are quick to blame others.
(A) Since
(B) During
(C) Although
(D) When

119. We need at least three days to _____ the genuineness of their intentions.
(A) assess
(B) assessing
(C) assessed
(D) assessment

120. During difficult times, the tension in people's bodies _____ mounting, making people uptight and exhausted.
(A) keeping
(B) keep
(C) keeps
(D) kept

121. In interpersonal communication, the first rule is to focus on listening to what _____ person wants to say.
(A) else
(B) some
(C) the other
(D) others

122. The first step in keeping customers is finding out _____ we lose customers.
(A) what
(B) why
(C) who
(D) when

123. The ideal leader demonstrates extreme professionalism combined _____ a warm humanity.
(A) to
(B) and
(C) for
(D) with

124. People tend to choose peace _____ conflict.
(A) over
(B) than
(C) to
(D) of

125. He is _____ for a career in business.
(A) impossible
(B) inconvenient
(C) unfit
(D) unclear

126. I'd like to talk to you today about an _____ development.
(A) excitement
(B) excited
(C) exciting
(D) excite

127. He always does a _____ piece of work.
(A) brisk
(B) virtuous
(C) timid
(D) careful

128. Many scientists believe that global warming is having a negative impact _____ the climate.
(A) for
(B) in
(C) of
(D) on

129. The secretary had all the _____ documents ready.
(A) relevant
(B) possible
(C) feasible
(D) reliable

130. This is the first time I have ever _____ to write such a long report.
(A) have
(B) had
(C) has
(D) having

Part VI. ► Text Completion

Directions: Read the texts that follow. A word or phrase is missing in some of the sentences. Four answer choices are given below each of these sentences. Select the best answer to complete the text. Then mark the letter (A), (B), (C), or (D) on your answer sheet.

Questions 131 - 134 refer to the following article.

A positive attitude is _____ in today's business world, and your choice of words is essential in

131. (A) growing
     (B) important
     (C) normal
     (D) attractive

creating the right attitude.

Now let's _____ these two statements: "My jobs are boring." / "My jobs could be more exciting

132. (A) compare
     (B) contradict
     (C) translate
     (D) develop

and my performance would be better if I could get more incentives." It is obvious _____ the first

133. (A) which
     (B) that
     (C) in which
     (D) it

statement is negative and reflects a passive attitude, whereas the second one is positive and reflects a desire to improve the situation.

Therefore, human resources department should develop strategies to motivate employees to think _____ and work hard.

134. (A) unfortunately
     (B) luckily
     (C) negatively
     (D) positively

Questions 135 - 138 refer to the following letter.

Dear Mr. Chen,

Our current supplier of first-grade paper _____ recently informed us that they are discontinuing

135. (A) has
(B) has been
(C) have
(D) had being

their first-grade paper division. So our purchasing director will be _____ some first-grade paper

136. (A) visits
(B) visit
(C) visiting
(D) visited

manufacturers in your area next month.

Would it be possible for you to arrange a meeting and plant tour for us _____ the 2nd or 3rd of

137. (A) on
(B) in
(C) of
(D) for

next month?

Enclosed please find data on our projected need for paper, production schedules, and delivery requirements. I hope the information may be helpful to you in _____ our visit. Thank you.

138. (A) preparing on
(B) prepare with
(C) preparing for
(D) prepared to

Sincerely,
Lucy Hung

Questions 139 - 142 refer to the following article.

In today's world of wanting things fast, customers don't want to call several different departments just to get a simple answer _____ the products they purchased.

139. (A) regarded
(B) regarding
(C) regards
(D) regard

Derma Corp., a leading cosmetic company, _____ this.

140. (A) respects
(B) memorizes
(C) remembers
(D) realizes

They are deploying a new system that will enable their customers to truly _____ a one call event

141. (A) experienced
(B) experience
(C) experiencing
(D) experiences

for all their questions.

Customers can simply make one call to place the order, check delivery, and handle other requests. This happens because Derma Corp. has an interactive database that links all of this information together _____ other divisions of the corporation.

142. (A) about
(B) to
(C) from
(D) since

Questions 143 - 146 refer to the following article.

This report is about "Will the Internet kill our magazines?" Well, that's true that new technologies change many things. _____ does the Internet really change everything?

        143. (A) If
            (B) But
            (C) And
            (D) So

People may surf, search, shop online, but they still read magazines. Based on our research, readership of our Beauty Magazine has actually _____ over the past two years.

        144. (A) increased
            (B) reported
            (C) accommodated
            (D) realized

Even the 17-to-29 segment _____ to grow. Rather than being displaced by instant media,

        145. (A) continue
            (B) continued
            (C) continues
            (D) continuing

magazines are still prevalent in people's life. The explanation is fairly _____. Magazines

        146. (A) skeptical
            (B) pessimistic
            (C) impersonal
            (D) obvious

promote deeper connections. They create relationships. They engage people in ways distinct from digital media. Magazines do what the Internet doesn't.

Part VII. ► Reading Comprehension

Directions: In this part you will read a selection of texts, such as magazine and newspaper articles, letters, and advertisements. Each text is followed by several questions. Select the best answer for each question and mark the letter (A), (B), (C), or (D) on your answer sheet.

Questions 147 - 148 refer to the following notice.

Investments in Malaysia as a Way to Make a Positive Impact

Invest Malaysia is an online microfinance platform. We believe micro and small enterprises have the potential to create jobs and sustainable economic growth. The best way to contribute to the success of these enterprises is to make investments in Malaysia. You can start investing with as little as $15! If you are ready to make a positive change, please visit www.invest-malaysia.com or call 123-3727-3746 to donate now.

147. What is the main purpose of this message?
   (A) To encourage investments in Malaysia
   (B) To report Malaysia's economic situation
   (C) To attract travelers to visit Malaysia
   (D) To explain how to start a business in Malaysia

148. What can be inferred about Invest Malaysia from the message?
   (A) It's the largest marketing research firm in Malaysia.
   (B) It has approximately 300 employees worldwide.
   (C) It's an online donation platform.
   (D) It helps companies to expand market.

Ambitious? Self-starter?

Are you tired of not making enough money?
Do you want to find the fastest way to get ahead?
Become a commissioned representative for Direct-Sales Co. today.

All you need is energy, passion, your own vehicle, and a telephone. And you can have an income of four, five, even six figures.

No salary, but a commission on every sale you make!

Visit our website www.direct-sales.com or call 123-3829-2382.

149. What is the main purpose of this advertisement?
(A) To recruit new sales representatives
(B) To attract new customers
(C) To propose new business opportunities
(D) To develop new product lines

150. The word "passion" in paragraph 2, line 1, is closest in meaning to
(A) performance
(B) management
(C) enthusiasm
(D) localization

151. What does the salesperson need to prepare in advance?
(A) A contract
(B) A website
(C) A car
(D) A laptop

Questions 152 - 153 refer to the following text message chain.

Carol	8:50 a.m.
Hi, Mark. Are you free now? I need to ask you something please. [1]	
Mark	9:10 a.m.
Sorry, Carol. I just returned to my seat. What's up? [2]	
Carol	9:11 a.m.
No problem. So what's the policy for vacation requests? Do you know?	
Mark	9:12 a.m.
You've got to submit an "Absent Request Form" to HR department first. So are you taking time off?	
Carol	9:15 a.m.
Yeah, I'll need to take a week off in July when kids are out of school. [3]	
Mark	9:16 a.m.
I see. You've been working hard and it's necessary to take a vacation to relax a bit. Well, anyway, if you have trouble filling out the form, feel free to send me a message.	
Carol	9:18 a.m.
Sure. [4] Thank you very much.	

152. At 9:10 a.m., why did Mark reply "Sorry, Carol. I just returned to my seat"?
   (A) To complain how busy he was
   (B) To explain the reason why he didn't reply earlier
   (C) To inform Carol that he's lost a case
   (D) To help Carol to get an absent request form

153. In which of the positions marked [1], [2], [3], and [4] does the following sentence best belong?
   "It's very kind of you."
   (A) [1]
   (B) [2]
   (C) [3]
   (D) [4]

Skinner Surgical Institute

Cosmetic surgery by internationally famous plastic surgeons.
Restore your youth, good looks, and self-confidence.

★ **Unsightly scars removed** ★
★ **Reshaping** ★
★ **Facial contouring** ★

Our clients have included leading figures from the worlds of entertainment, politics, and business.

Email today for our free brochure filled with "Before and After" photographs and testimonials:
info@skinner.com or call 123-3828-3284.

154. What is the purpose of the advertisement?
(A) To encourage foreign investment
(B) To advertise a cosmetic clinic
(C) To recommend a change in the law
(D) To support cooperation with other clinics

155. What is suggested about doing cosmetic surgery?
(A) It is a newly developed surgery.
(B) It will increase your self-confidence.
(C) It is not as costly as you expected.
(D) It is limited to women only.

156. The word "testimonial" in the last paragraph, line 1, is closest in meaning to
(A) innovation
(B) management
(C) endorsement
(D) education

Questions 157 - 159 refer to the following article.

Ability to change is critical in the business environment

– An exclusive interview with Mr. William Bosch of Best Systems

Best Systems is a software company which survived the dot-com crash of the late 90s. As William Bosch, its CEO, recalls, "By that time, we had already redirected our business. We focused mainly on our target markets, so we were concentrating on enterprise customers who really cared about the quality of the IT system they used."

"Our mission hasn't changed," Mr. Bosch adds, "It's always been about developing, designing, marketing, selling software to help enterprises to reduce IT problems and costs." The company has gone through various transformations. One involved changing the way they did business. The second involved focusing on new products. And the third involved moving forward to new customer bases.

But as Mr. Bosch recognizes, the key to successful change is the people working for the company. "It was important that our employees felt proud about what they were doing, and they believed what they were doing was having an impact on the world."

157. How did Best Systems survive the dot-com crash?
(A) They took on a new CEO.
(B) They reduced the size of the company.
(C) They changed direction before it happened.
(D) They announced new product lines.

158. What is Best Systems' main objective?
(A) To become the best market research firm
(B) To diversify their product types
(C) To recruit the most ambitious employees
(D) To make software products to improve customers' IT environments

159. According to Mr. Bosch, what has motivated Best Systems' employees?
(A) The highest pay in the industry
(B) The way Best Systems' products are making a difference
(C) The variety of hardware products they make
(D) The new lifestyle they are creating

Questions 160 - 161 refer to the following letter.

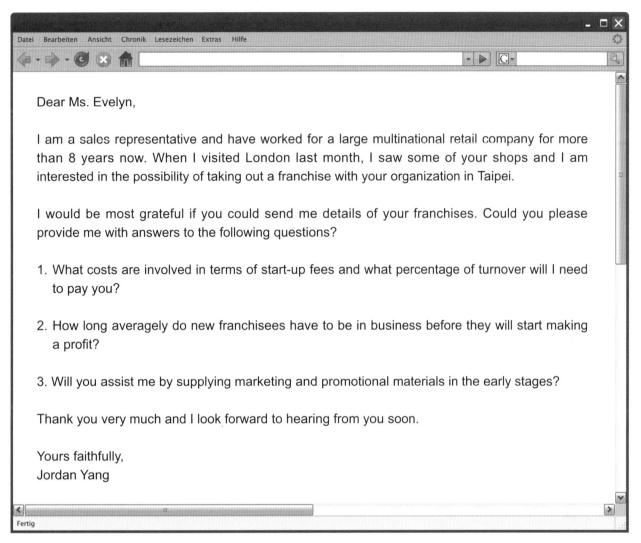

Dear Ms. Evelyn,

I am a sales representative and have worked for a large multinational retail company for more than 8 years now. When I visited London last month, I saw some of your shops and I am interested in the possibility of taking out a franchise with your organization in Taipei.

I would be most grateful if you could send me details of your franchises. Could you please provide me with answers to the following questions?

1. What costs are involved in terms of start-up fees and what percentage of turnover will I need to pay you?

2. How long averagely do new franchisees have to be in business before they will start making a profit?

3. Will you assist me by supplying marketing and promotional materials in the early stages?

Thank you very much and I look forward to hearing from you soon.

Yours faithfully,
Jordan Yang

160. What is the purpose of this letter?
(A) To inquire about partnership opportunity
(B) To promote a new product
(C) To advertise a new organization
(D) To recommend a change in marketing strategy

161. The word "grateful" in paragraph 2, line 1, is closest in meaning to
(A) thankful
(B) patient
(C) automatic
(D) demanding

Questions 162 - 164 refer to the following notice.

Registration for Network Summit in Springfield, California, July 25-29, is now open.

The summit is the premier partner training conference on network work style solutions, encompassing mobility, cloud networking, and social collaboration. This event will provide strategy, intensive training and new tools to help you take advantage of the huge business potential in the mobile work style market space.

See what's new for 2018!

Free pre-event lab training: Attendees who have paid their summit registration by July 10th will receive online access to Self-paced Learning Labs on July 22nd

Beautiful new location: Enjoy the vibes of sunny California and the elegance of the Rainbow Convention Center

Preview summit content:

Previews of breakout sessions across all three tracks – **Mobility, Cloud, and Networking** – are now available. The full session catalog will launch in May.

In addition to breakouts, the comprehensive summit agenda offers activities ranging from keynotes by Network CEO John Lewis and members of his executive team to the Partner Solutions Center showcasing resources, programs and tools.

Get ready for an exciting venue, a schedule packed with technical training and exceptional value that starts before the event itself.

We hope you will join us at Network Summit.

162. What is this article about?
(A) A summit invitation
(B) A hotel reservation confirmation
(C) An interview schedule
(D) A competition announcement

163. Why should participants pay registration fees by July 10th?
(A) To get a 10% discount
(B) To get a free copy of the software
(C) To attend an online training
(D) To join a celebration party

164. What is NOT mentioned as a main track of the summit?
(A) Networking
(B) Mobility
(C) Cloud
(D) Productivity

Questions 165 - 167 refer to the following letter.

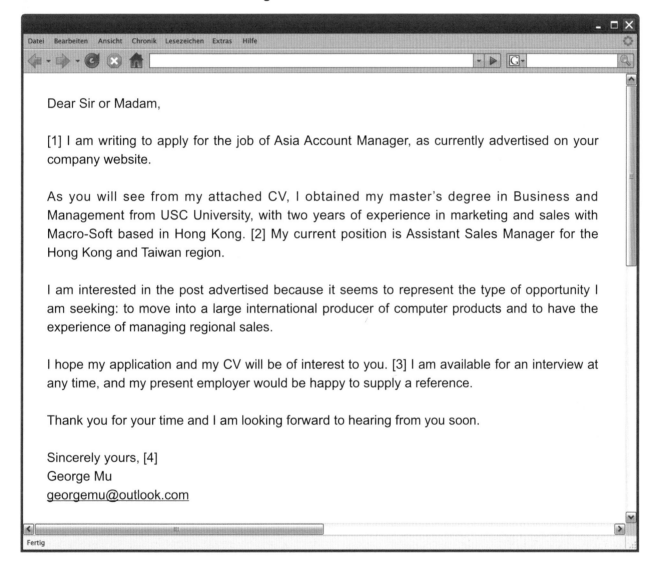

Dear Sir or Madam,

[1] I am writing to apply for the job of Asia Account Manager, as currently advertised on your company website.

As you will see from my attached CV, I obtained my master's degree in Business and Management from USC University, with two years of experience in marketing and sales with Macro-Soft based in Hong Kong. [2] My current position is Assistant Sales Manager for the Hong Kong and Taiwan region.

I am interested in the post advertised because it seems to represent the type of opportunity I am seeking: to move into a large international producer of computer products and to have the experience of managing regional sales.

I hope my application and my CV will be of interest to you. [3] I am available for an interview at any time, and my present employer would be happy to supply a reference.

Thank you for your time and I am looking forward to hearing from you soon.

Sincerely yours, [4]
George Mu
georgemu@outlook.com

165. What does George Mu say about his job expectation?
(A) He would like to transfer to the US.
(B) He wants to lead a group of software developers.
(C) He would like to work in an international environment.
(D) He wants to return to school for advanced courses.

166. What is being sent with the letter?
(A) A design sample
(B) George Mu's resume
(C) George Mu's diploma
(D) A reference letter

167. In which of the positions marked [1], [2], [3], and [4] does the following sentence best belong?

"I would like to meet you in person and demonstrate that I do have the ability to achieve company goals."

(A) [1]

(B) [2]

(C) [3]

(D) [4]

Questions 168 - 171 refer to the following article.

Visiting Taipei

Taipei 101

Taipei 101 is one of the world's tallest skyscrapers. It is situated in Taipei's business district. It has 101 stories above the ground and 5 stories underground. The building is designed to withstand earthquakes and typhoons. It claims official records for the fastest ascending elevator.

Night Market

Night markets in Taipei serve a wide variety of delicious and inexpensive food. People from all over the world come here to taste the mouth-watering food. The small stalls of variety of food items open at 4 p.m. and close at around 1 or 2 in the morning.

Zhong-Xiao E. Road

Zhong-Xiao E. Road is known as a popular entertainment and retail area with numerous shopping malls and department stores located along most of the entire stretch. It is one of the most modern and stylish areas of Taipei. Visitors can shop for whatever they desire in this road.

168. Where would this piece of information most likely appear?

(A) In a user's manual

(B) In a newspaper

(C) In a Taiwan travel guide

(D) On Zhong-Xiao E. Road

169. What is NOT mentioned about Taipei 101?

(A) It's one of the skyscrapers in the world.

(B) It's located in the business district.

(C) There is a night market inside.

(D) It's a 101-story building.

170. What time do night markets usually open?

(A) 4 p.m.

(B) 1 a.m.

(C) 2 p.m.

(D) 4 a.m.

171. What is mentioned about Zhong-Xiao E. Road in the article?

(A) There are only a few shopping malls here.

(B) It's a modern area of Taipei.

(C) People come here to eat inexpensive food.

(D) This place is full of high-technology companies.

Questions 172 - 175 refer to the following letter.

To: HR Director
From: Sales and Marketing
Subject: Re: Training Session

Hello Mr. Carson,

After all sales and marketing staff attended the recent training on "productive meetings", some have expressed dissatisfaction with the training. There are two major reasons for that and I suppose you should be aware of those.

First of all, our staff felt that the content was not related to the actual meetings that staff have to attend in their work. Instead, the training seemed to be just a standard course on meetings in general. Therefore, several team members thought that it was not helpful at all.

Secondly, there was no time left for our team members to ask questions. This also meant that there was no solid connection between the training itself and the actual meetings.

We think it is important for our members to feel that we are addressing their training needs, isn't it? Therefore, I suggest we look into the possibility of using a different trainer in the future. New trainers should provide us with an outline of the course so we can ensure the training will accurately address staff needs.

Please feel free to call me at extension 111, if you have any other thoughts or feedbacks. Thank you.

Lily Chang

172. Why does Lily Chang write this email?
  (A) To complain about a training course
  (B) To thank the HR Director for his help
  (C) To ask for more training information
  (D) To request some product samples

173. Who is most likely Lily Chang?
  (A) Mr. Carson's assistant
  (B) HR Director
  (C) Marketing Manager
  (D) Company CEO

174. What problem does Lily mention about the training?
(A) Employees still don't know how to hold meetings.
(B) Some team members were absent.
(C) It was a dull training.
(D) It is not relevant to the actual situation.

175. What does Lily suggest?
(A) Ask team members to give more feedback.
(B) Give the current trainer another opportunity.
(C) Change a new trainer next time.
(D) Call extension 111 for more suggestions.

Questions 176 - 180 refer to the following article and letter.

Restaurant Review

The ideas for Good-Diner new limited-time offer sandwiches came from its dining rooms. For years, Good-Diner guests have been seen stacking steak between cheese toast and stuffing shrimp into split dinner rolls. Now, Good-Diner is doing the work for their guests.

Three all-new sandwiches are putting Good-Diner's signature steak, seafood and chicken into guests' hands. The new sandwich, covered in BBQ sauce and topped with hand-breaded onion straws, is served on a freshly baked French roll.

"Sandwiches are growing in popularity with consumers," said Chef Tony Baker. "We've always been known for our steak, seafood and salads. We may need to change that to steak, seafood, salads and sandwiches."

Good-Diner's new sandwiches are available at all locations from today.

About Good-Diner
From choice steaks cut fresh in-house every day, to salads, soups and baked goods – all created in our own kitchens – Good-Diner is where customers come for great food. Famous for over thirty appetizers, soups, salads and dessert bar, guests enjoy the flexibility of dining at their own pace, with servers delivering meals and clearing tables.

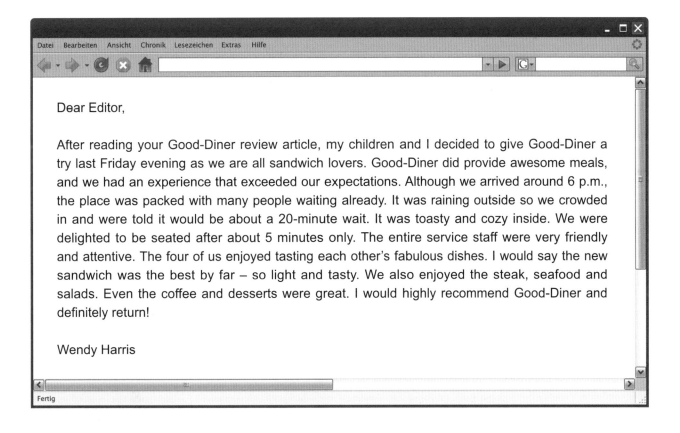

Dear Editor,

After reading your Good-Diner review article, my children and I decided to give Good-Diner a try last Friday evening as we are all sandwich lovers. Good-Diner did provide awesome meals, and we had an experience that exceeded our expectations. Although we arrived around 6 p.m., the place was packed with many people waiting already. It was raining outside so we crowded in and were told it would be about a 20-minute wait. It was toasty and cozy inside. We were delighted to be seated after about 5 minutes only. The entire service staff were very friendly and attentive. The four of us enjoyed tasting each other's fabulous dishes. I would say the new sandwich was the best by far – so light and tasty. We also enjoyed the steak, seafood and salads. Even the coffee and desserts were great. I would highly recommend Good-Diner and definitely return!

Wendy Harris

176. Where does the article most likely appear?
   (A) In a magazine
   (B) In a dictionary
   (C) In a phone directory
   (D) In a textbook

177. What kind of food is NOT served in this restaurant?
   (A) Sandwiches
   (B) Steak
   (C) Salads
   (D) Beef noodles

178. What is the main idea of the letter?
   (A) Good-Diner is a high-end restaurant and very expensive.
   (B) Good-Diner mainly serves pizza.
   (C) The restaurant is way too crowded.
   (D) Good-Diner is truly a restaurant worth trying.

179. Who is Wendy Harris?
   (A) A satisfied customer of Good-Diner
   (B) A mother of four children
   (C) A magazine editor
   (D) A chef at Good-Diner

180. How long did it take for Wendy to be seated?
   (A) 20 minutes
   (B) 5 minutes
   (C) 10 minutes
   (D) Half an hour

Questions 181 - 185 refer to the following letters.

August 25th, 2018

Luke White
Soft-Tech Co.
1837 Cedar Lane
Hackney, VA 38282

Dear Mr. White,

We are interested in software applications used in virtualization IT environments. As you are one of the leading software vendors, we would greatly appreciate receiving more information, brochures and price lists you may have to learn more about your software products and virtualization solutions. Please send such materials to:

Attention: Jenny Thomas
ICS Inc.
1849 Heart Street
Hackney, VA 38389

Thank you in advance and I am looking forward to studying the materials you send.

Sincerely,
Jenny Thomas
Technical Coordinator, ICS Inc.

August 30th, 2018

Ms. Jenny Thomas
ICS Inc.
1849 Heart Street
Hackney, VA 38389

Dear Ms. Thomas,

Thank you for your interest in our virtualization products and solutions. After reviewing our brochures and materials, I'm confident that you will be pleased with our solutions and the benefits our products can offer.

Allow me to mention some points which I'm confident will interest you.

We offer enterprises <u>executive mobility</u>: Our virtualization solutions enable your employees to work with people, data, and applications from the latest devices — anywhere.

Employees can work under the latest "<u>bring-your-own device</u>" model: Our products make high-level managers embrace personalization, empower employees, and simplify IT infrastructures.

We also ensure <u>security and compatibility</u> of various devices: With our solutions, enterprises can secure confidential business information while maximizing access and collaboration.

I will be pleased to address any questions or concerns you may have. Please feel free to call me at 123-2374-3828 if there is anything I can do for you.

Thank you.

Sincerely,
Luke White

181. What is the purpose of Jenny Thomas' letter?
   (A) To request more information about an IT solution
   (B) To apply for a technical support engineer position
   (C) To poach talents from Luke White's company
   (D) To invite Luke White to attend an IT seminar

182. What can be inferred about Soft-Tech Co.?
   (A) It's a newly established company.
   (B) Its stock price is very high.
   (C) It's a leading company providing virtualization solutions.
   (D) Its CEO is going to retire soon.

183. What is probably being sent with the second
letter?
(A) A meeting agenda
(B) Soft-Tech's product brochure
(C) Successful customer stories
(D) A conference invitation

184. What is NOT mentioned in Luke White's letter
as a product feature?
(A) Mobility
(B) BYOD model
(C) Security
(D) Low prices

185. What should Jenny Thomas do if she has
more questions?
(A) Call Luke White
(B) Check on the website
(C) Do more research
(D) Read some manuals

Questions 186 - 190 refer to the following website, notice, and table.

Great-Hill Annual User Conference

Registration & Attendance

Registration Policy	On-Site Check-in	Hotel Accommodations

This year's Great-Hill User Conference will make our clients experience comprehensive learning and networking opportunities.

- Hands-on sessions: training sessions led by industry experts
- Exploration zone: a place to explore the newest technologies with touch screen demos and interactive learning
- Discussion room: allowing clients to schedule one-on-one appointments with experts
- Client appreciation event: great opportunities to network with your peers
- Executive forum: an invitation-only event with sessions and activities designed for C-level executives

Click here for FAQs

Great-Hill Annual User Conference FAQs

Question: **Do I need to be a Great-Hill user to attend the conference?**

Answer: No. While there will be technology-development-focused discussions, this is not the only benefit of the conference. Anyone interested in technology development and the topic of software design would benefit from the presentations and group discussions. The Great-Hill Annual User Conference is a place for Great-Hill users, and those interested in technology development. For conference agenda, please refer to the following chart.

Question: **What if I don't currently use Great-Hill solutions, but have an interest in the software and potential to use it in the future?**

Answer: The Great-Hill AUC is the perfect conference to explore the software and learn how it can be used to benefit your company. It is a great time to take advantage of a low-cost Great-Hill training ($100.00) and we will be happy to supply prospective users with a temporary version (30-day trial license) of the software at no charge to participate and explore using the software.

Question: **Are there discounts available for multiple registrations?**

Answer: Yes. Please contact Lucy Graw at 123-3736-3846 or lucy.graw@great-hill.com to inquire about discounts for registering multiple participants from one company.

Question: **What is the dress code for the conference?**

Answer: Business casual attire is requested for the event.

Great-Hill Annual User Conference Agenda

Friday, March 30ᵗʰ, 2018

07:30 AM – 08:30 AM	**Registration and Breakfast**
08:30 AM – 08:45 AM	**Dr. Judith Tyrie** Opening Remarks
08:45 AM – 10:15 AM	**Kim Lee, UC University, Professor of Computer Science** Technology Development in the Future
10:15 AM – 10:45 AM	**Break**
10:45 AM – 11:15 AM	**George Rosa, Great-Hill Inc., Vice President, Engineering** Big Data Analytics
11:15 AM – 12:00 PM	**Terry Johnson, EAU Corp., Strategic Consultant** Technology and Innovation
12:00 PM – 01:00 PM	**Lunch**
01:00 PM – 02:00 PM	**Session A: Computer Network Hands-on Lab**
01:00 PM – 02:00 PM	**Session B: Virtualization Solutions**
02:00 PM – 03:00 PM	**Panel Discussion: Tech Trends**
03:00 PM – 03:30 PM	**Break**
03:30 PM – 04:15 PM	**Dr. Bill Thomson, Scientific Thailand Corp.** Successful Case Studies
04:15 PM – 05:00 PM	**Albert Black, Great-Hill Inc., CEO** Closing Remarks

186. According to the webpage information, which is NOT mentioned as a session of the conference?
(A) Outdoor activities
(B) Hands-on labs
(C) 1:1 Discussion
(D) Appreciation party

187. What is the purpose of the FAQs?
(A) To report on a competition for students
(B) To list questions and answers that participants might have
(C) To announce an upcoming event
(D) To advertise a computer game show

188. For whom are these three pieces of information probably intended?
(A) University professors
(B) Conference participants
(C) Projector manufacturers
(D) Conference organizers

190. According to the agenda, when can attendees choose between different topics?
(A) 1 p.m.
(B) 2 p.m.
(C) 10 a.m.
(D) 4 p.m.

189. What can be inferred about Ms. Lucy Graw?
(A) She is one of the speakers.
(B) She will arrange travels for attendees.
(C) She handles the group discount issue.
(D) She is in charge of creating the event website.

Questions 191 - 195 refer to the following letters.

Datei   Bearbeiten   Ansicht   Chronik   Lesezeichen   Extras   Hilfe

From: Gina Lo [ginalo@mail.com]
To: Mark Wu [mark-wu@ilt.com]
Subject: Marketing Specialist Position
Date: July 6, 2018

Dear Mr. Wu,

Thank you for taking the time out of your busy schedule to discuss with me about the Marketing Specialist with ILT Research Company. I really appreciate your time and consideration in interviewing me for this position.

After speaking with you and the group, I am confident that I would be a right and perfect candidate for this position. In addition to my educational background and excellent English communication ability, I would bring the marketing and strategic thinking necessary to get the job done.

I am very interested in working for you and looking forward to hearing from you once the final decisions are made regarding this Marketing Specialist position. Please feel free to contact me at any time if further information is needed. I can be reached at 0948-383-3838.

Thank you again for your time and consideration.

Sincerely,
Gina Lo

Fertig

July 15th, 2018

Ms. Gina Lo
1128 Good Road
Taipei, Taiwan, 104

Dear Ms. Lo,

It was my pleasure to meet with you on June 17th, 2018. I was pretty impressed with your abilities and skills. Your qualifications are what our company is looking for and we are delighted to offer you the position of Marketing Specialist at ILT Research Co. I am certain you will be pleased with the benefits the position and our company provide.

Please allow me to outline the terms of our offer. Your monthly salary is NT$45,000, with yearly bonuses tied to your division's net sales. In addition, you will have three weeks of vacation time per year and ten sick days. We would like you to be on board on Wednesday, August 15th.

You will receive the following training courses for the first two weeks:
– Understanding customer behaviors
– Using analysis tools to interpret data
– Consolidating research results

Please contact me by August 5th so that we can confirm your acceptance of this offer. Welcome to ILT Research Co. and we are looking forward to working with you soon.

Sincerely,
Mark Wu

July 17th, 2018

Mr. Mark Wu
ILT Research Co.
4737 Business Ave.
Taipei, Taiwan, 100

Dear Mr. Wu,

I am happy to accept the position as Marketing Specialist in your department. The training program outlined in your letter convinced me that your company offers excellent growth opportunities for its marketing staff.

I understand that my salary will begin at NT$45,000 per month and I hope that my immediate supervisor will consider a salary increase when I demonstrate more expertise after I join your team.

The start date of August 15th is acceptable and I look forward to thanking you in person when we meet in your office on that date.

Sincerely,
Gina Lo

191. Why does Gina write the email to Mark Wu?
(A) To sell him some new products
(B) To follow up on her previous interview
(C) To invite Mark Wu for a lunch meeting
(D) To arrange another interview with Mark Wu

192. What can be inferred about Gina Lo from these letters?
(A) She will start to work at ILT in a month.
(B) She is a software developer.
(C) She is not experienced enough for the job.
(D) She will relocate to a new branch in September.

193. In the second letter, the word "interpret" in paragraph 3, line 3, is closest in meaning to
(A) continue
(B) terminate
(C) communicate
(D) elucidate

194. What should Gina Lo do by August 5th?
(A) Submit her application form
(B) Contact Mark Wu to confirm the job offer
(C) Schedule an interview with Mark Wu
(D) Attend a training session

195. What does Gina Lo mention about ILT?
(A) They should expand their product line.
(B) Their managers should give employees a pay raise.
(C) They offer valuable training courses to help staff grow.
(D) Their main entrance needs a facelift.

Questions 196 - 200 refer to the following emails.

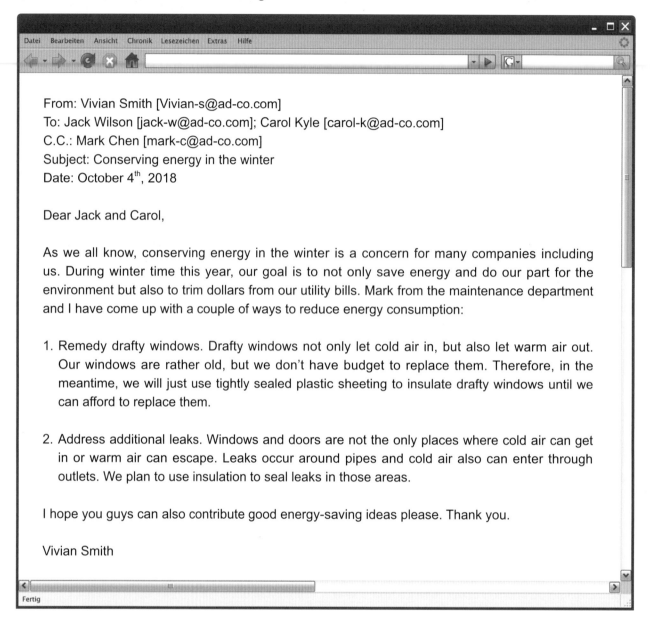

From: Vivian Smith [Vivian-s@ad-co.com]
To: Jack Wilson [jack-w@ad-co.com]; Carol Kyle [carol-k@ad-co.com]
C.C.: Mark Chen [mark-c@ad-co.com]
Subject: Conserving energy in the winter
Date: October 4th, 2018

Dear Jack and Carol,

As we all know, conserving energy in the winter is a concern for many companies including us. During winter time this year, our goal is to not only save energy and do our part for the environment but also to trim dollars from our utility bills. Mark from the maintenance department and I have come up with a couple of ways to reduce energy consumption:

1. Remedy drafty windows. Drafty windows not only let cold air in, but also let warm air out. Our windows are rather old, but we don't have budget to replace them. Therefore, in the meantime, we will just use tightly sealed plastic sheeting to insulate drafty windows until we can afford to replace them.

2. Address additional leaks. Windows and doors are not the only places where cold air can get in or warm air can escape. Leaks occur around pipes and cold air also can enter through outlets. We plan to use insulation to seal leaks in those areas.

I hope you guys can also contribute good energy-saving ideas please. Thank you.

Vivian Smith

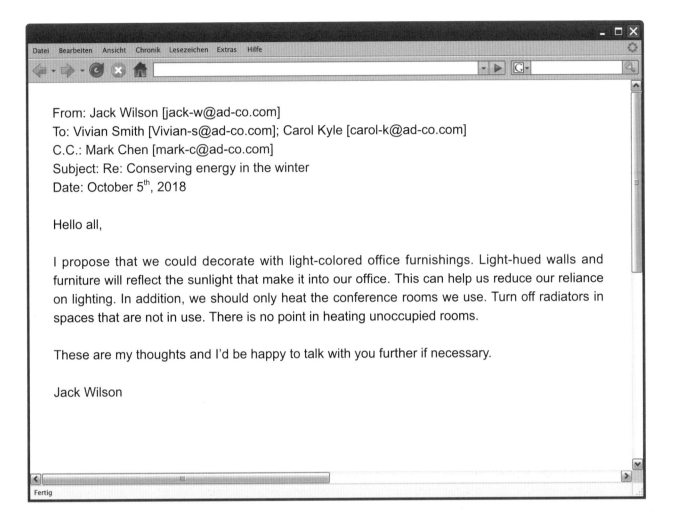

From: Jack Wilson [jack-w@ad-co.com]
To: Vivian Smith [Vivian-s@ad-co.com]; Carol Kyle [carol-k@ad-co.com]
C.C.: Mark Chen [mark-c@ad-co.com]
Subject: Re: Conserving energy in the winter
Date: October 5th, 2018

Hello all,

I propose that we could decorate with light-colored office furnishings. Light-hued walls and furniture will reflect the sunlight that make it into our office. This can help us reduce our reliance on lighting. In addition, we should only heat the conference rooms we use. Turn off radiators in spaces that are not in use. There is no point in heating unoccupied rooms.

These are my thoughts and I'd be happy to talk with you further if necessary.

Jack Wilson

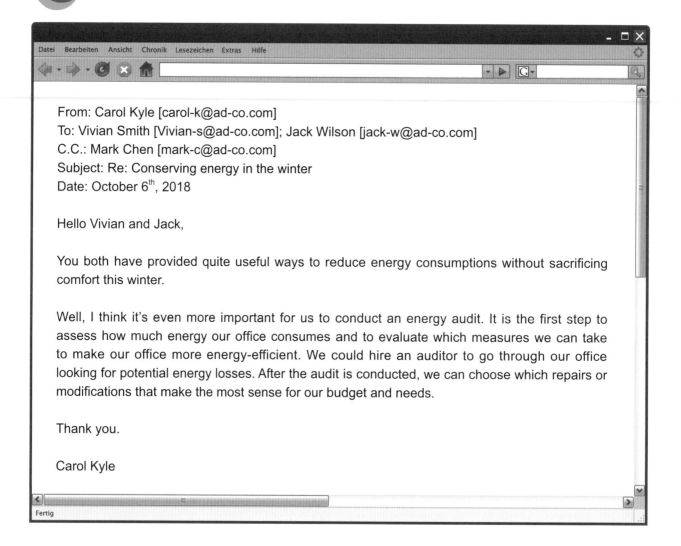

From: Carol Kyle [carol-k@ad-co.com]
To: Vivian Smith [Vivian-s@ad-co.com]; Jack Wilson [jack-w@ad-co.com]
C.C.: Mark Chen [mark-c@ad-co.com]
Subject: Re: Conserving energy in the winter
Date: October 6th, 2018

Hello Vivian and Jack,

You both have provided quite useful ways to reduce energy consumptions without sacrificing comfort this winter.

Well, I think it's even more important for us to conduct an energy audit. It is the first step to assess how much energy our office consumes and to evaluate which measures we can take to make our office more energy-efficient. We could hire an auditor to go through our office looking for potential energy losses. After the audit is conducted, we can choose which repairs or modifications that make the most sense for our budget and needs.

Thank you.

Carol Kyle

196. In the first email, the word "conserve" in paragraph 1, line 1, is closest in meaning to
    (A) discuss
    (B) sustain
    (C) squander
    (D) consume

197. Why does Vivian write the email to other colleagues?
    (A) To ask them to submit sales reports
    (B) To discuss the progress of a project
    (C) To inform them of an event in winter
    (D) To discuss some energy-saving ideas

198. What is Jack's proposal?
    (A) To use light-colored furnishings
    (B) To replace all the old windows
    (C) To turn on air conditioners
    (D) To recycle plastic bottles

199. What does Carol proposal doing first?
    (A) Hold a meeting to discuss tomorrow
    (B) Prepare marketing materials earlier
    (C) Conduct an energy audit in advance
    (D) Hire more sales reps first

200. Which is NOT mentioned as a way to conserve energy in these emails?
(A) Seal windows tightly
(B) Resolve leaking problems
(C) Turn off heaters in unused rooms
(D) Hold an energy-saving competition

考前準備系列　TP207

新多益一本通【模擬試題】

出版及發行／師德文教股份有限公司
台北市忠孝西路一段 100 號 12 樓
TEL: (02) 2382-0961　FAX: (02) 2382-0841
http://www.cet-taiwan.com

總　編　輯／邱靖媛
作　　　者／文之勤
執行編輯／王清雪
文字編輯／林怡婷
美術編輯／林淑慧
封面設計／林雅蓁

總經銷／紅螞蟻圖書有限公司
台北市內湖區舊宗路二段 121 巷 19 號
TEL: (02) 2795-3656　FAX: (02) 2795-4100
E-mail: red0511@ms51.hinet.net
特約門市／敦煌書局全省連鎖門市

登記證／行政院新聞局局版臺業字第 288 號
印刷者／金瓚印刷事業有限公司
初版／2018 年 6 月

◉ 版權所有‧翻印必究 ◉
購書時如有缺頁或破損，請寄回更換。謝謝！